## THE FOLGER LIBRARY
## SHAKESPEARE

Designed to make Shakespeare's classic plays available to the general reader, each edition contains a reliable text with modernized spelling and punctuation, scene-by-scene plot summaries, and explanatory notes clarifying obscure and obsolete expressions. An interpretive essay and accounts of Shakespeare's life and theater form an instructive preface to each play.

Louis B. Wright, General Editor, was the Director of the Folger Shakespeare Library from 1948 until his retirement in 1968. He is the author of *Middle-Class Culture in Elizabethan England, Religion and Empire, Shakespeare for Everyman,* and many other books and essays on the history and literature of the Tudor and Stuart periods.

Virginia Lamar, Assistant Editor, served as research assistant to the Director and Executive Secretary of the Folger Shakespeare Library from 1946 until her death in 1968. She is the author of *English Dress in the Age of Shakespeare* and *Travel and Roads in England,* and coeditor of William Strachey's *Historie of Travell into Virginia Britania.*

*The Folger Shakespeare Library*

*The Folger Library General Reader's Shakespeare*

# THE
# MERCHANT
## OF
# VENICE

by
## WILLIAM
## SHAKESPEARE

WASHINGTON SQUARE PRESS
PUBLISHED BY POCKET BOOKS NEW YORK

A Washington Square Press Publication of
POCKET BOOKS, a division of Simon & Schuster, Inc.
1230 Avenue of the Americas, New York, N.Y 10020

ISBN: 0-671-49178-4

First Pocket Books printing November, 1957

45  44  43  42  41  40

WASHINGTON SQUARE PRESS, WSP and colophon are
registered trademarks of Simon & Schuster, Inc.

Printed in the U.S.A.

# *Preface*

This edition of *The Merchant of Venice* is designed to make available a readable text of one of Shakespeare's greatest plays. In the centuries since Shakespeare many changes have occurred in the meanings of words, and some clarification of Shakespeare's vocabulary may be helpful. To provide the reader with necessary notes in the most accessible format, we have placed them on the pages facing the text that they explain. We have tried to make these notes as brief and simple as possible. Preliminary to the text we have also included a brief statement of essential information about Shakespeare and his stage. Readers desiring more detailed information should refer to the books suggested in the references, and if still further information is needed, the bibliographies in those books will provide the necessary clues to the literature of the subject.

L. B. W.
V. A. L.

*April 5, 1957*

# THE QUALITY OF
## *The Merchant of Venice*

THE TITLE PAGE of the earliest printed version of *The Merchant of Venice,* the quarto of 1600, announced that it had been "divers times acted" by Shakespeare's company of players. The date of the first performance is unknown but it probably took place sometime in 1596. After the accession of King James I, the company performed the play at court in February, 1605, and pleased the King so well that he ordered a second performance. There are no further records of performance in this period. The Puritans, who controlled England from 1640 to 1660, regarded theatres as schoolhouses of the devil and in 1642 forbade the acting of plays altogether. When the theatres reopened in 1660, some of Shakespeare's plays were performed, but *The Merchant of Venice* is not recorded among them. An adaptation was made by George Granville and performed in 1701. This version held the stage until 1741, when the original play was again produced, this time at Drury Lane. From that day to this, *The Merchant of Venice* has been one of Shakespeare's most popular plays, both on the stage and as a reading text.

The reasons for the popularity of the play must be found in the quality of the poetry, the clarity of the characterization, and the romantic elements that

*Lopez compounding to poyson the Queens.*

From G. Carleton, A Thankfull Remembrancer (1674).

transcend the darker aspects of the treatment of Shylock. Shakespeare is dealing with the themes of Love and Hate, and Love comes out supreme in the person of Portia, one of the most attractive of Shakespeare's heroines. The delineation of Portia, more than any other factor, probably accounts for the enduring charm of *The Merchant of Venice*.

The characterization of Shylock has troubled thoughtful students of Shakespeare, who have wondered at the apparent anti-Semitism in his portrayal. The question at once is asked whether Shakespeare is writing from life and is deliberately picturing in an unfavorable light a character he might have seen on the streets of London. Numerous writers have discussed the existence of Jews in Elizabethan England and the contemporary attitude toward them without coming to agreement. Sir Sidney Lee and Lucien Wolf have argued that Shakespeare could have known converted Jews in London and that a considerable number of refugees from Spain and Portugal lived in England as converts or practiced their religion in secret. J. L. Cardozo in *The Contemporary Jew in the Elizabethan Drama* has given convincing proof that so few Jews were known in Shakespeare's England that he could not have been drawing Shylock's picture from any living prototype. To be sure, there was the case of the unfortunate Portuguese Jewish physician Dr. Roderigo Lopez, who was executed in June, 1594, for allegedly plotting against the life of Queen Elizabeth, but Lopez was a convert and if he suffered from prejudice at his trial it reflected the normal Elizabethan prejudice against foreigners, particularly Latins, and was not a result of his Jewish blood. The notion that Shakespeare wrote *The Mer-*

*chant of Venice* to capitalize on the interest in the Lopez case has little substantiation.

In making Shylock, the moneylender, a member of the Jewish race, Shakespeare was not consciously contributing to anti-Semitism, but he was reflecting a cruelty that persisted from past ages of persecution. In the early Middle Ages, the Jews had occupied a place of economic importance in England as bankers and moneylenders. Periodically they suffered persecution, and in 1290 Edward I expelled them from his kingdom. They were not legally admitted again to England until Cromwell relaxed the laws in 1655 and 1656. To justify their cruelty to the Jews, Christians invented libels that are still familiar, including the tales of ritual murder, one of which Chaucer repeats in the Hugh of Lincoln story. A stereotype of a "wicked Jew" got into the stream of literature throughout Western Europe and became a convention.

In the biblical drama that played such a great part in the religious festivals of the Middle Ages and lasted until Shakespeare's boyhood, the character of Judas Iscariot was conventionalized as the embodiment of this type of wickedness. When the medieval dramatist wanted to illustrate the ultimate in iniquity, he found in Judas a character made to order for his purpose. As the biblical drama became more debased in popular performance, Judas evolved into a low-comedy part. He was inevitably costumed in a red wig, red beard, and a huge nose. At a high moment in the play, children might beat him off the pageant wagon and send him roaring through the streets, where he and the devils in the drama engaged in much comic buffoonery.

The English public was conditioned to this representation of Judas both as a figure of towering wickedness and as a clown. When Marlowe wanted to portray a character of consummate evil, he remembered the dramatic tradition of Judas and created Barabas in *The Jew of Malta,* a play that may have influenced Shakespeare. But Marlowe in painting Barabas' portrait was not thinking of any person living in England; he was merely drawing on the common reservoir of literary types. From the earlier days of persecution there was a tradition of using the Jew for a whipping boy, a tradition perpetuated in literature and folklore, which Shakespeare merely followed. It is significant that Shylock was portrayed on the stage until the nineteenth century in the conventional "Judas" costume of red wig, red beard, and large nose. The theatrical conventions of the Middle Ages died hard.

But Shakespeare was an artist of extraordinary power, and he was not content to represent Shylock merely as a symbol of evil. As always in his plays, the dramatist gives his characters life, and Shylock, who might have become merely the representation of an abstract vice in the hands of a lesser dramatist, becomes in Shakespeare's re-creation a man who has suffered much, whose hatred is explained by the treatment he and his whole race have had to endure. He is the symbol of Hate, it is true, but Hate induced by injustice and humiliation.

The interpretation of Shylock on the stage in modern times has varied with the taste and judgment of actors. Some followed the older tradition and treated Shylock as a comic part; others played him sympathetically. In the early nineteenth century, Edmund Kean played Shylock with such pathos that spectators wept over his great speech in which he asked, "Hath not a Jew eyes? Hath not a Jew hands, organs, dimensions, senses, affections, passions?"

Shakespeare derived the main outlines of the plot of *The Merchant of Venice* from an Italian collection of short stories entitled *Il Pecorone*, by Ser Giovanni Fiorentino. Put together in the late fourteenth century, it was first printed in Italian in 1558. At the time Shakespeare wrote his play, no English translation, so far as we know, had yet been made. Shakespeare got the story either from the original Italian or from some intermediary source, possibly from an older play. From the Italian story comes the Jewish creditor demanding a pound of flesh from the Christian who defaults on his debt. The theme of the three caskets may derive from another old collection of stories, the *Gesta Romanorum,* and two or three other sources may account for elements in the play not traceable to *Il Pecorone*. As always, Shakespeare worked over old material and created something fresh and new with his particular mark of genius upon it.

The characters in *The Merchant of Venice* stand out as personalities even when they serve as symbols. Shylock will always be remembered as a human being, though Shakespeare may have intended him to stand for Hate. Portia is a vivid girl who wins the admiration of every man, though Shakespeare may have intended her to stand for the abstraction of Love. Antonio is a living Elizabethan, a pensive, melancholy fellow whom Shakespeare may have numbered among his friends, even though he represents the principle of Noble Friendship so treasured in this period. The lesser characters—Bassanio, Gratiano, Jessica, Nerissa, even the

# THE
# EXCELLENT

## History of the Merchant of Venice.

With the extreme cruelty of *Shylocke*
the Iew towards the saide Merchant, in cutting a iust pound of his flesh. And the obtaining
of *Portia*, by the choyse of
*three Caskets*.

Written by W. SHAKESPEARE.

Printed by *J. Roberts*, 1600.

The title page of the First Quarto of *The Merchant of Venice*.

clown, Launcelot Gobbo—all have human traits that make them interesting as individuals, a quality that has made *The Merchant of Venice* a favorite play for actors. All of the parts are something more than cardboard figures in a pantomime.

Despite the dark shadow cast by Shylock's purposed revenge, the play has gaiety and lightness. The audience knows that Antonio is not really going to forfeit a pound of flesh and die; it guesses that his ships have not foundered irrevocably; and by the standards of the Elizabethan age, it is a work of virtue that Portia circumvents Shylock, who, willy-nilly, becomes a Christian, and that Jessica is made happy with a Christian husband. To an Elizabethan, it was all a charming fairy tale with a happy ending and they could share Lorenzo's contentment as he sat with Jessica on the terrace at Belmont:

> How sweet the moonlight sleeps upon this bank!
> Here will we sit and let the sounds of music
> Creep in our ears. Soft stillness and the night
> Become the touches of sweet harmony.

With moonlight and music the play closes, and we hear the muted laughter of lovers who have found their way to each other's arms and have still a jest to share.

## THE TEXT OF THE PLAY

*The Merchant of Venice* first appeared in print in 1600 in a quarto version. This First Quarto provides a good text and most modern editions are based upon it.

A second quarto appeared in 1619 with a fraudulent date of 1600 given as the date of publication. This reprints the First Quarto and has no textual authority of its own. The First Folio text of the play also reprints the First Quarto, with variant readings, many of which correct confusing or erroneous passages in the earlier text. The present edition uses the First Quarto but includes approximately fifty readings from the Folio which represent corrections of the First Quarto text. Several readings suggested by later editors have been adopted as indicated in the notes.

Neither the Folio nor the Quarto text contains settings for the various scenes, and stage directions are few and inadequate. Accordingly, settings and stage directions have been added to illuminate the action. These and additions to directions adopted from the original texts are enclosed in square brackets. The Folio text provides division of the play into acts but the scene divisions have been devised by modern editors.

The numbering of lines is literally line by line and therefore does not agree with the lineation in most concordances, which follow the convention of counting two consecutive half-lines of verse as one metrical line.

## THE AUTHOR

BY THE TIME *The Merchant of Venice* first appeared in print, Shakespeare was so well known as a literary and dramatic craftsman that Francis Meres, a young preacher, in a volume called *Palladis Tamia: Wits Treasury* (1598), referred in flattering terms to him as "mellifluous and honey-tongued Shakespeare," famous for his *Venus and Adonis,* his *Lucrece,* and "his sugared sonnets," which were circulating "among his private friends." Meres observes further that "as Plautus and Seneca are accounted the best for comedy and tragedy among the Latins, so Shakespeare among the English is the most excellent in both kinds for the stage," and he mentions a dozen plays that had made a name for Shakespeare. He concludes with the remark "that the Muses would speak with Shakespeare's fine filed phrase if they would speak English."

To those acquainted with the history of the Elizabethan and Jacobean periods, it is incredible that anyone should be so naïve or ignorant as to doubt the reality of Shakespeare as the author of the plays that bear his name. Yet so much nonsense has been written about other "candidates" for the plays that it is well to remind readers that no credible evidence that would stand up in a court of law has ever been adduced to prove either that Shakespeare did not write his plays or that anyone else wrote them. All the theories offered for the authorship of Francis Bacon, the Earl of Derby, the Earl of Oxford, the Earl of Hertford, Christopher Marlowe, and a score of other candidates are mere conjectures spun from the active imaginations of persons who confuse hypothesis and conjecture with evidence.

As Meres' statement of 1598 indicates, Shakespeare was already a popular playwright whose name carried weight at the box office. The obvious reputation of Shakespeare as early as 1598 makes the effort to prove him a myth one of the most absurd in the history of human perversity.

The anti-Shakespeareans talk darkly about a plot of vested interests to maintain the authorship of Shakespeare. Nobody has any vested interest in Shakespeare, but every scholar is interested in the truth and in the quality of evidence advanced by special pleaders who set forth hypotheses in place of facts.

The anti-Shakespeareans base their arguments upon a few simple premises all of them false. These false premises are that Shakespeare was an unlettered yokel without any schooling, that nothing is known about Shakespeare and that only a noble lord or the equivalent in background could have written the plays. The facts are that more is known about Shakespeare than about most dramatists of his day, that he had a very good education acquired in the Stratford Grammar School that the plays show no evidence of profound book learning and that the knowledge of kings and courts evident in the plays is no greater than any intelligent young man could have picked up at second hand. Most anti-Shakespeareans are naïve and betray an obvious snobbery. The author of their favorite plays, they imply must have had a college diploma framed and hung on his study wall like the one in their dentist's office, and obviously so great a writer must have had a title or some equally significant evidence of exalted social background. They forget that genius has a way of cropping up in unexpected places and that none of the great creative writers of the world got his inspiration in a college or university course.

William Shakespeare was the son of John Shakespeare of Stratford-upon-Avon, a substantial citizen of that small but busy market town in the center of the rich agricultural county of Warwick. John Shakespeare kept a shop, what we would call a general store; he dealt in wool and other produce and gradually acquired property. As a youth, John Shakespeare had learned the trade of glover and leather worker. There is no contemporary evidence that the elder Shakespeare was a butcher, though the anti-Shakespeareans like to talk about the ignorant "butcher's boy of Stratford." Their only evidence is a statement by gossipy John Aubrey, more than a century after William Shakespeare's birth, that young William followed his father's trade and when he killed a calf "he would do it in a high style and make a speech." We would like to believe the story true, but Aubrey is not a very credible witness.

John Shakespeare probably continued to operate a farm at Snitterfield that his father had leased. He married Mary Arden, daughter of his father's landlord, a man of some property. The third of their eight children was William, baptized on April 26, 1564, and probably born three days before. At least it is conventional to celebrate April 23 as his birthday.

The Stratford records give considerable information about John Shakespeare. We know that he held several municipal offices including those of alderman and mayor. In 1580 he was in some sort of legal difficulty and was fined for neglecting a summons of the Court of Queen's Bench requiring him to appear at Westminster and be bound over to keep the peace.

As a citizen and alderman of Stratford, John Shakespeare was entitled to send his son to the grammar school free. Though the records are lost, there can be no reason to doubt that this is where young William received his education. As any student of the period knows, the grammar schools provided the basic education in Latin learning and literature. The Elizabethan grammar school is not to be confused with modern grammar schools. Many cultivated men of the day received all their formal education in the grammar schools. At the universities in this period a student would have received little training that would have inspired him to be a creative writer. At Stratford young Shakespeare would have acquired a familiarity with Latin and some little knowledge of Greek. He would have read Latin authors and become acquainted with the plays of Plautus and Terence. Undoubtedly in this period of his life he received that stimulation to read and explore for himself the world of ancient and modern history which he later utilized in his plays. The youngster who does not acquire this type of intellectual curiosity *before* college days rarely develops as a result of a college course the kind of mind Shakespeare demonstrated His learning in books was anything but profound. but he clearly had the probing curiosity that sent him in search of information, and he had a keenness in the observation of nature and of humankind that finds reflection in his poetry.

There is little documentation for Shakespeare's boyhood. There is little reason why there should be. Nobody knew that he was going to be a dramatist about whom any scrap of information would be prized in the centuries to come. He was merely an active and vigorous youth of Stratford, perhaps assisting his father in his business, and no Boswell bothered to write down facts about him. The most important record that we have is a marriage license issued by the Bishop of Worcester on November 28, 1582, to permit William Shakespeare to marry Anne Hathaway, seven or eight years his senior; furthermore, the Bishop permitted the marriage after reading the banns only once instead of three times, evidence of the desire for haste. The need was explained on May 26, 1583, when the christening of Susanna, daughter of William and Anne Shakespeare, was recorded at Stratford. Two years later, on February 2, 1585, the records show the birth of twins to the Shakespeares, a boy and a girl who were christened Hamnet and Judith.

What William Shakespeare was doing in Stratford during the early years of his married life, or when he went to London, we do not know. It has been conjectured that he tried his hand at school teaching, but that is a mere guess. There is a legend that he left Stratford to escape a charge of poaching in the park of Sir Thomas Lucy of Charlecote, but there is no proof of this. There is also a legend that when first he came to London, he earned his living by holding horses outside a playhouse and presently was given employment inside, but there is nothing better than eighteenth-century hearsay for this. How Shakespeare broke into the London theatres as a dramatist and actor, we do not know. But lack of information is not surprising, for Elizabethans did not write their autobiographies, and we know even less about the lives of many writers and some men of affairs than we know about Shakespeare. By 1592 he was so well established and popular that he incurred the envy of the dramatist and pamphleteer Robert Greene, who referred to him as an "upstart crow . . . in his own conceit the only Shakescene in a country." From this time onward contemporary allusions and references in legal documents enable the scholar to chart Shakespeare's career with greater accuracy than is possible with most other Elizabethan dramatists.

By 1594 Shakespeare was a member of the company of actors known then as the Lord Chamberlain's Men. After the accession of James I, in 1603, the company would have the sovereign for their patron and would be known as the King's Men. During the period of its greatest prosperity, this company would have as its principal theatres the Globe and the Blackfriars. Shakespeare was both an actor and a shareholder in the company. He thus had three sources of income: from the sale of his plays to the company, from his wages as an actor, and from his share of the profits of the theatrical company. Tradition has assigned him such acting roles as Adam in *As You Like It* and the Ghost in *Hamlet*, a modest place on the stage that suggests that he may have had other duties in the management of the company. Such conclusions, however, are based on surmise.

What we do know is that his plays were popular and that he was highly successful in his triple vocation. His first play may have been *The Comedy of Errors*, acted perhaps in 1591. Certainly this was one of his earliest plays. The three parts of *Henry VI* were acted sometime between 1590 and 1592. Critics are not in agreement about precisely how much Shakespeare wrote of these three plays. *Richard III* probably dates from 1593. With this play Shakespeare captured the imagination of Elizabethan audiences, then enormously interested in historical plays. With *Richard III*, Shakespeare also gave an interpretation pleasing to the Tudors of the rise to power of the grandfather of Queen Elizabeth. From this time onward, Shakespeare's plays followed on the stage in rapid succession: *Titus Andronicus, The Taming of the Shrew, The Two Gentlemen of Verona, Love's Labour's Lost, Romeo and Juliet, Richard II,*

*A Midsummer Night's Dream, King John, The Merchant of Venice, Henry IV,* Pts. I and II, *Much Ado About Nothing, Henry V, Julius Caesar, As You Like It, Twelfth Night, Hamlet, The Merry Wives of Windsor, All's Well That Ends Well, Measure for Measure, Othello, King Lear,* and nine others that followed before Shakespeare retired completely, about 1613.

In the course of his career in London, he made enough money to enable him to retire to Stratford with a competence. His purchase on May 4, 1597, of New Place, then the second largest dwelling in Stratford, a "pretty house of brick and timber," with a handsome garden, indicates his increasing prosperity. There his wife and children lived while he busied himself in the London theatres. The summer before he acquired New Place, his life was darkened by the death of his only son, Hamnet, a child of eleven. In May, 1602, Shakespeare purchased one hundred and seven acres of fertile farmland near Stratford and a few months later bought a cottage and garden across the alley from New Place. About 1611, he seems to have returned permanently to Stratford, for the next year a legal document refers to him as "William Shakespeare of Stratford-upon-Avon . . . gentleman." To achieve the desired appellation of gentleman, William Shakespeare had seen to it that the College of Heralds in 1596 granted his father a coat of arms. In one step he thus became a second-generation gentleman.

Shakespeare's daughter Susanna made a good match in 1607 with Dr. John Hall, a prominent and prosperous Stratford physician. His second daughter, Judith, did not marry until she was thirty-two years old, and then, under somewhat scandalous circumstances, she married Thomas Quiney, a Stratford vintner. On March 25, 1616, Shakespeare made his will, bequeathing his landed property to Susanna, £300 to Judith, certain sums to other relatives, and his second-best bed to his wife Anne. Much has been made of the second-best bed, but the legacy probably indicates only that Anne liked that particular bed. Shakespeare, following the practice of the time, may have already arranged with Susanna for his wife's care. Finally, on April 23, 1616, the anniversary of his birth, William Shakespeare died, and he was buried on April 25 within the chancel of Trinity Church, as befitted an honored citizen. On August 6, 1623, a few months before the publication of the collected edition of Shakespeare's plays, Anne Shakespeare joined her husband in death.

## THE PUBLICATION OF HIS PLAYS

DURING HIS LIFETIME Shakespeare made no effort to publish any of his plays, though eighteen appeared in print in single-play editions known as quartos. Some of these are corrupt versions known as "bad quartos." No quarto, so far as is known, had the author's approval. Plays were not considered "literature" any more than radio and television scripts today are considered literature. Dramatists sold their plays outright to the theatrical companies and it was usually considered in the company's interest to keep plays from getting into print. To achieve a reputation as a man of letters, Shakespeare wrote his *Sonnets* and his narrative poems, *Venus and Adonis* and *The Rape of Lucrece*, but he probably never dreamed that his plays would establish his reputation as a literary genius. Only Ben Jonson, a man known for his colossal conceit, had the crust to call his plays *Works,* as he did when he published an edition in 1616. But men laughed at Ben Jonson.

After Shakespeare's death, two of his old colleagues in the King's Men, John Heming and Henry Condell, decided that it would be a good thing to print, in more accurate versions than were then available, the plays already published and eighteen additional plays not previously published in quarto. In 1623 appeared *Mr. William Shakespeares Comedies, Histories, & Tragedies. Published according to the True Originall Copies. London. Printed by Isaac Iaggard and Ed. Blount.* This was the famous First Folio, a work that had the authority of Shakespeare's associates. The only play commonly attributed to Shakespeare that was omitted in the First Folio was *Pericles.* In their preface, "To the great Variety of Readers," Heming and Condell state that whereas "you were abused with diverse stolen and surreptitious copies, maimed and deformed by the frauds and stealths of injurious impostors that exposed them, even those are now offered to your view cured and perfect of their limbs; and all the rest, absolute in their numbers, as he conceived them." What they used for printer's copy is one of the vexed problems of scholarship, and skilled bibliographers have devoted years of study to the question of the relation of the "copy" for the First Folio to Shakespeare's manuscripts. In some cases it is clear that the editors corrected printed quarto versions of the plays, probably by comparison with playhouse scripts. Whether these scripts were in Shakespeare's autograph is anybody's guess. No manuscript of any play in Shakespeare's handwriting has survived. Indeed, very few play manuscripts from this period by any author are extant. The Tudor and Stuart periods had not yet learned to prize autographs and authors' original manuscripts.

Since the First Folio contains eighteen plays not previously printed, it is the only source for these. For the other eighteen, which had appeared in quarto versions, the First Folio also has the authority of an edition prepared and overseen by Shakespeare's colleagues and professional associates. But since editorial standards in 1623 were far from strict, and Heming and Condell were actors rather than editors by profession, the texts are sometimes careless. The printing and proofreading of the First Folio also left much to be desired, and some garbled passages have to be corrected and emended. The "good quarto" texts have to be taken into account in preparing a modern edition.

Because of the great popularity of Shakespeare through the centuries the First Folio has become a prized book, but it is not a very rare one, for it is estimated that 238 copies are extant. The Folger Shakespeare Library in Washington, D.C., has seventy-nine copies of the First Folio, collected by the founder, Henry Clay Folger, who believed that a collation of as many texts as possible would reveal significant facts about the text of Shakespeare's plays. Dr. Charlton Hinman, using an ingenious machine of his own invention for mechanical collating, has made many discoveries that throw light on Shakespeare's text and on printing practices of the day.

The probability is that the First Folio of 1623 had an edition of between 1,000 and 1,250 copies. It is believed that it sold for £1, which made it an expensive book, for £1 in 1623 was equivalent to something between $40 and $50 in modern purchasing power.

During the seventeenth century, Shakespeare was sufficiently popular to warrant three later editions in folio size, the Second Folio of 1632, the Third Folio of 1663-1664, and the Fourth Folio of 1685. The Third Folio added six other plays ascribed to Shakespeare, but these are apocryphal.

## THE SHAKESPEAREAN THEATRE

THE THEATRES in which Shakespeare's plays were performed were vastly different from those we know today. The stage was a platform that jutted out into the area now occupied by the first rows of seats on the main floor, what is called the "orchestra" in America and the "pit" in England. This platform had no curtain to come down at the ends of acts and scenes. And although simple stage properties were available, the Elizabethan theatre lacked both the machinery and the elaborate movable scenery of the modern theatre. In the rear of the platform stage was a curtained area that could be used as an inner room, a tomb, or any such scene that might be required. A balcony above this inner room, and perhaps balconies on the sides of the stage, could represent the upper deck of a ship, the entry to Juliet's room, or a prison window. A trap door in the stage provided an entrance for ghosts and devils from the nether regions, and a similar trap in the canopied structure over the stage, known as the "heavens," made it possible to let down angels on a rope. These primitive stage arrangements help to account for many elements in Elizabethan plays. For example, since there was no curtain, the dramatist frequently felt the necessity of writing into his play action to clear the stage at the ends of acts and scenes. The funeral march at the end of *Hamlet* is not there merely for atmosphere; Shakespeare had to get the corpses off the stage. The lack of scenery also freed the dramatist from undue concern about the exact location of his sets, and the physical relation of his various settings to each other did not have to be worked out with the same precision as in the modern theatre.

Before London had buildings designed exclusively for theatrical entertainment, plays were given in inns and taverns. The characteristic inn of the period had an inner courtyard with rooms opening onto balconies overlooking the yard. Players could set up their temporary stages at one end of the yard and audiences could find seats on the balconies out of the weather. The poorer sort could stand or sit on the cobblestones in the yard, which was open to the sky. The first theatres followed this construction, and throughout the Elizabethan period the large public theatres had a yard in front of the stage open to the weather, with two or three tiers of covered balconies extending around the theatre. This physical structure again influenced the writing of plays. Because a dramatist wanted the actors to be heard, he frequently wrote into his play orations that could be delivered with declamatory effect. He also provided spectacle, buffoonery, and broad jests to keep the riotous groundlings in the yard entertained and quiet.

In another respect the Elizabethan theatre differed greatly from ours. It had no actresses. All women's roles were taken by boys, sometimes recruited from the boys' choirs of the London churches. Some of these youths acted their roles with great skill and the Elizabethans did not seem to be aware of any incongruity. The first actresses on the professional English stage appeared after the Restoration of Charles II, in 1660, when exiled Englishmen brought back from France practices of the French stage.

London in the Elizabethan period, as now, was the center of theatrical interest, though wandering actors from time to time traveled through the country performing in inns, halls, and the houses of the nobility. The first professional playhouse, called simply The Theatre, was erected by James Burbage, father of Shakespeare's colleague Richard Burbage, in 1576 on lands of the old Holywell Priory adjacent to Finsbury Fields, a playground and park area just north of the city walls. It had the advantage of being outside the city's jurisdiction and yet was near enough to be easily accessible. Soon after The Theatre was opened, another playhouse called The Curtain was erected in the same neighborhood. Both of these playhouses had open courtyards and were probably polygonal in shape.

About the time The Curtain opened, Richard Farrant, Master of the Chapel Royal at Windsor and of St. Paul's, conceived the idea of opening a "private" theatre in the old monastery buildings of the Blackfriars, not far from St. Paul's Cathedral in the heart of the city. This theatre was ostensibly to train the choirboys in plays for presentation at Court. Actually, Farrant managed to present plays to paying audiences and achieved considerable success until aristocratic neighbors complained and had the theatre closed. This first Blackfriars

Theatre was significant, however, because it popularized the boy actors in a professional way and it paved the way for a second theatre in the Blackfriars, which Shakespeare's company took over more than thirty years later. By the last years of the sixteenth century, London had at least six professional theatres and still others were erected during the reign of James I.

The Globe Theatre, the playhouse that most people connect with Shakespeare, was erected early in 1599 on the Bankside, the area across the Thames from the city. Its construction had a dramatic beginning, for on the night of December 28, 1598, James Burbage's sons, Cuthbert and Richard, gathered together a crew who tore down the old theatre in Holywell and carted the timbers across the river to a site that they had chosen for a new playhouse. The reason for this clandestine operation was a row with the landowner over the lease to the Holywell property. The site chosen for the Globe was another playground outside of the city's jurisdiction, a region of somewhat unsavory character. Not far away was the Bear Garden, an amphitheatre devoted to the baiting of bears and bulls. This was also the region occupied by many houses of ill fame licensed by the Bishop of Winchester and the source of substantial revenue to him. But it was easily accessible either from London Bridge or by means of the cheap boats operated by the London watermen, and it had the great advantage of being beyond the authority of the Puritanical aldermen of London, who frowned on plays because they lured apprentices from work, filled their heads with improper ideas, and generally exerted a bad influence. The aldermen also complained that the crowds drawn together in the theatre helped to spread the plague.

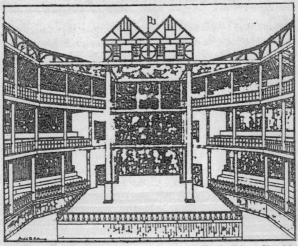

A reconstruction of the stage of the Globe Playhouse.
From Joseph Quincy Adams,
*A Life of William Shakespeare* (1923).

The Globe was the handsomest theatre up to its time.
It was a large octagonal building, open like its predeces-
sors to the sky in the center, but capable of seating a
large audience in its covered balconies. To erect and
operate the Globe, the Burbages organized a syndicate
composed of the leading members of the dramatic company, of which Shakespeare was a member. Since it
was open to the weather and depended on natural light,
plays had to be given in the afternoon. This caused no
hardship in the long afternoons of an English summer,
but in the winter the weather was a great handicap
and discouraged all except the hardiest. For that reason,

in 1608 Shakespeare's company was glad to take over the lease of the second Blackfriars Theatre, a substantial, roomy hall reconstructed within the framework of the old monastery building. This theatre was protected from the weather and its stage was artificially lighted by chandeliers of candles. This became the winter play-house for Shakespeare's company and at once proved so popular that the congestion of traffic created an embarrassing problem. Stringent regulations had to be made for the movement of coaches in the vicinity. Shakespeare's company continued to use the Globe during the summer months. In 1613 a squib fired from a cannon during a performance of *Henry VIII* fell on the thatched roof and the Globe burned to the ground. The next year it was rebuilt.

London had other famous theatres. The Rose, just west of the Globe, was built by Philip Henslowe, a semiliterate denizen of the Bankside, who became one of the most important theatrical owners and producers of the Tudor and Stuart periods. What is more important for historians, he kept a detailed account book, which provides much of our information about theatrical history in his time. Another famous theatre on the Bankside was the Swan, which a Dutch priest, Johannes de Witt, visited in 1596. The crude drawing of the stage which he made was copied by his friend Arend van Buchell; it is one of the important pieces of contemporary evidence for theatrical construction. De Witt described the Swan as capable of holding three thousand spectators. Among the other theatres, the Fortune, north of the city, on Golding Lane, and the Red Bull, even farther away from the city, off St. John's Street, were the most popular. The Red Bull, much frequented by apprentices, favored sensational and sometimes rowdy plays.

The actors who kept all of these theatres going were organized into companies under the protection of some noble patron. Traditionally actors had enjoyed a low reputation. In some of the ordinances they were classed as vagrants; in the phraseology of the time, "rogues, vagabonds, sturdy beggars, and common players" were all listed together as undesirables. To escape penalties often meted out to these characters, organized groups of actors managed to gain the protection of various personages of high degree. In the later years of Elizabeth's reign, a group flourished under the name of the Queen's Men; another group had the protection of the Lord Admiral and were known as the Lord Admiral's Men. Edward Alleyn, son-in-law of Philip Henslowe, was the leading spirit in the Lord Admiral's Men. Besides the adult companies, troupes of boy actors from time to time also enjoyed considerable popularity. Among these were the Children of Paul's and the Children of the Chapel Royal.

The company with which Shakespeare had a long association had for its patron Henry Carey, Lord Hunsdon, the Lord Chamberlain, and hence they were known as the Lord Chamberlain's Men. After the accession of James I, they became the King's Men. This company was the great rival of the Lord Admiral's Men, managed by Henslowe and Alleyn.

All was not easy for the players in Shakespeare's time, for the aldermen of London were always eager for an excuse to close up the Blackfriars and any other theatres in their jurisdiction. The theatres outside the jurisdiction of London were not immune from interference, for they might be shut up by order of the Privy Council for meddling in politics or for various other offenses, or they might be closed in time of plague lest they spread infection. During plague times, the actors usually went on tour and played the provinces wherever they could find an audience. Particularly frightening were the plagues of 1592-1594 and 1613 when the theatres closed and the players, like many other Londoners, had to take to the country.

Though players had a low social status, they enjoyed great popularity and one of the favorite forms of entertainment at Court was the performance of plays. To be commanded to perform at Court conferred great prestige upon a company of players, and printers frequently noted that fact when they published plays. Many of Shakespeare's plays were performed before the sovereign and Shakespeare himself undoubtedly acted in some of these plays.

## References for Further Reading

MANY READERS will want suggestions for further reading about Shakespeare and his times. The literature in this field is enormous but a few references will serve as guides to further study. A simple and useful little book is Gerald Sanders, *A Shakespeare Primer* (New York, 1950). *A Companion to Shakespeare Studies*, edited by Harley Granville-Barker and G. B. Harrison (Cambridge, Eng., 1934) is a valuable guide. More detailed but still not too voluminous to be confusing is Hazelton Spencer, *The Art and Life of William Shakespeare* (New York, 1940) which, like Sanders' handbook, contains a brief annotated list of useful books on various aspects of the subject. The most detailed and scholarly work providing complete factual information about Shakespeare is Sir Edmund Chambers, *William Shakespeare: A Study of Facts and Problems* (2 vols., Oxford, 1930). For detailed, factual information about the Elizabethan and seventeenth-century stages, the definitive reference works are Sir Edmund Chambers, *The Elizabethan Stage* (4 vols., Oxford, 1923) and Gerald E. Bentley, *The Jacobean and Caroline Stage* (5 vols., Oxford, 1941–1956). Alfred Harbage, *Shakespeare's Audience* (New York, 1941) throws light on the nature and tastes of the customers for whom Elizabethan dramatists wrote.

Although specialists disagree about details of stage

construction, the reader will find essential information in John C. Adams, *The Globe Playhouse: Its Design and Equipment* (Barnes & Noble, 1961). A model of the Globe playhouse by Dr. Adams is on permanent exhibition in the Folger Shakespeare Library in Washington, D.C. An excellent description of the architecture of the Globe is Irwin Smith, *Shakespeare's Globe Playhouse: A Modern Reconstruction in Text and Scale Drawings Based upon the Reconstruction of the Globe by John Cranford Adams* (New York, 1956). Another recent study of the physical characteristics of the Globe is C. Walter Hodges, *The Globe Restored* (London, 1953). An easily read history of the early theatres is J. Q. Adams, *Shakespearean Playhouses: A History of English Theatres from the Beginnings to the Restoration* (Boston, 1917).

The following titles on theatrical history will provide information about Shakespeare's plays in later periods: Alfred Harbage, *Theatre for Shakespeare* (Toronto, 1955); Esther Cloudman Dunn, *Shakespeare in America* (New York, 1939; George C. D. Odell, *Shakespeare from Betterton to Irving* (2 vols., London, 1931); Arthur Colby Sprague, *Shakespeare and the Actors: The Stage Business in His Plays (1660–1905)* (Cambridge, Mass., 1944) and *Shakespearian Players and Performances* (Cambridge, Mass., 1953); Leslie Hotson, *The Commonwealth and Restoration Stage* (Cambridge, Mass., 1928); Alwin Thaler, *Shakspere to Sheridan: A Book About the Theatre of Yesterday and To-day* (Cambridge, Mass., 1922); Ernest Bradlee Watson, *Sheridan to Robertson: A Study of the 19th-Century London Stage* (Cambridge, Mass., 1926). Enid Welsford, *The Court Masque* (Cambridge, Mass., 1927) is an excellent study of the characteristics of this form of entertainment.

Harley Granville-Barker, *Prefaces to Shakespeare* (5 vols., London, 1927–1948) provides stimulating critical discussion of the plays. An older classic of criticism is Andrew C. Bradley, *Shakespearean Tragedy: Lectures on Hamlet, Othello, King Lear, Macbeth* (London, 1904), which is now available in an inexpensive reprint (New York, 1955). Thomas M. Parrot, *Shakespearean Comedy* (New York 1949) is scholarly and readable. Shakespeare's dramatizations of English history are examined in E. M. W. Tillyard, *Shakespeare's History Plays* (London, 1948), and Lily Bess Campbell, *Shakespeare's "Histories," Mirrors of Elizabethan Policy* (San Marino, Calif., 1947) contains a more technical discussion of the same subject.

Reprints of some of the sources of Shakespeare's plays can be found in *Shakespeare's Library* (2 vols., 1850), edited by John Payne Collier, and *The Shakespeare Classics* (12 vols., 1907–1926), edited by Israel Gollancz. Geoffrey Bullough, *Narrative and Dramatic Sources of Shakespeare* (New York, 1957) is a new series of volumes reprinting the sources. Two volumes covering the early comedies, comedies (1597–1603), and histories are now available. For discussion of Shakespeare's use of his sources see Kenneth Muir, *Shakespeare's Sources: Comedies and Tragedies* (London, 1957). Thomas M. Cranfill has recently edited a facsimile reprint of *Riche His Farewell to Military Profession* (1581), which contains stories that Shakespeare probably used for several of his plays.

A refutation of the contention that Jews were well known in Elizabethan England is contained in J. L.

Cardozo, *The Contemporary Jew in the Elizabethan Drama* (Amsterdam, 1925). Treatises that take the opposite point of view are Sidney Lee, *Elizabethan England and the Jew,* published in the Transactions of the New Shakespeare Society (London, 1888), and Lucien Wolf, "Jews in Elizabethan England," in The Jewish Historical Society of England, *Transactions, Sessions 1924–1927* (London, 1928), 1-91.

Interesting pictures as well as new information about Shakespeare will be found in F. E. Halliday, *Shakespeare, a Pictorial Biography* (London, 1956). Allardyce Nicoll, *The Elizabethans* (Cambridge, Eng., 1957) contains a variety of illustrations.

A brief, clear. and accurate account of Tudor history is S. T. Bindoff, *The Tudors,* in the Penguin series. A readable general history is G. M. Trevelyan, *The History of England,* first published in 1926 and available in many editions. G. M. Trevelyan, *English Social History,* first published in 1942 and also available in many editions, provides fascinating information about England in all periods. Sir John Neale, *Queen Elizabeth* (London, 1934) is the best study of the great Queen. Various aspects of life in the Elizabethan period are treated in Louis B. Wright, *Middle-Class Culture in Elizabethan England* (Chapel Hill, N.C., 1935; reprinted by Cornell University Press, 1958). *Shakespeare's England: An Account of the Life and Manners of His Age,* edited by Sidney Lee and C. T. Onions (2 vols., Oxford, 1916), provides a large amount of information on many aspects of life in the Elizabethan period. Additional information will be found in Muriel St. C. Byrne, *Elizabethan Life in Town and Country* (Barnes & Noble, 1961).

[*Dramatis Personae.*

*The Duke of Venice.*
*The Prince of Morocco,* } suitors to *Portia.*
*The Prince of Arragon,*

*Antonio,* a merchant of Venice.
*Bassanio,* his friend, suitor likewise to *Portia.*
*Solanio,*
*Salerio,* } friends to *Antonio* and *Bassanio.*
*Gratiano,*

*Lorenzo,* in love with *Jessica.*
*Shylock,* a Jew.
*Tubal,* a Jew, his friend.
*Launcelot Gobbo,* a clown, servant to *Shylock.*
*Old Gobbo,* father to *Launcelot.*
*Leonardo,* servant to *Bassanio.*
*Balthasar,*
*Stephano,* } servants to *Portia.*

*Portia,* an heiress.
*Nerissa,* her waiting gentlewoman.
*Jessica,* daughter to *Shylock.*

Magnificoes, Officers, Jailer, Servants, and other
  Attendants.

SCENE.—*Venice and Belmont.*]

# THE
# MERCHANT
## OF
# VENICE

# ACT I

**I.** [i.] Antonio, the "Merchant of Venice," promises to lend his friend Bassanio, who is nobly born but penniless, the money necessary to finance his suit for the hand of Portia, the beautiful and wealthy heiress of Belmont. Since all of Antonio's money is tied up in commercial ventures, Bassanio sets out to borrow on Antonio's credit.

▪▪▪▪▪▪▪▪▪▪▪▪▪▪▪▪▪▪▪▪▪▪▪▪▪▪▪

1. **sooth:** truth

5. **am to learn:** have yet to find out

9. **argosies:** "merchant ships," originally meaning "ships of Ragusa," an Adriatic port, the sixteenth-century name of which was Arragosa; **portly:** swelled by the wind, inflated, probably with the secondary meaning "majestic"

11. **pageants:** floats, similar to those in modern parades, which were used in processions through the streets and sometimes on rivers such as the Thames

12. **overpeer the petty traffickers:** look down upon lesser craft

17. **still:** continually

18. **Plucking the grass to know where sits the wind:** picking blades of grass and throwing them up to see which way the wind will blow them

19. **Piring:** peering

# ACT I

[Scene I. A street in Venice.]

Enter *Antonio, Salerio,* and *Solanio.*

*Ant.* In sooth, I know not why I am so sad.
It wearies me; you say it wearies you;
But how I caught it, found it, or came by it,
What stuff 'tis made of, whereof it is born,
I am to learn;                                                    5
And such a want-wit sadness makes of me
That I have much ado to know myself.
  *Saler.* Your mind is tossing on the ocean;
There where your argosies with portly sail—
Like signiors and rich burghers on the flood,              10
Or, as it were, the pageants of the sea—
Do overpeer the petty traffickers,
That curtsy to them, do them reverence,
As they fly by them with their woven wings.
  *Solan.* Believe me, sir, had I such venture forth,      15
The better part of my affections would
Be with my hopes abroad. I should be still
Plucking the grass to know where sits the wind,
Piring in maps for ports, and piers, and roads;

I

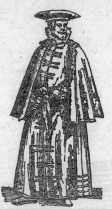

A Venetian merchant of the sixteenth century.
From Jean de Glen, *Des Habits, Moeurs, etc.* (1601).

21. **out of doubt:** doubtless, certainly

24. **blow me to an ague:** give me a chill

28. **"Andrew":** a ship's name. An English expedition to Cádiz in 1596 captured a Spanish galleon named the "St. Andrew." Salerio's use of the name is probably a topical allusion.

29. **Vailing:** bowing in homage; the whole phrase describes the ship heeling over so that her mast touches the ground.

32. **straight:** at once

36-7. **but even now worth this,/ And now worth nothing:** one moment worth this much, the next moment worthless

43. **one bottom:** one ship

And every object that might make me fear          20
Misfortune to my ventures, out of doubt
Would make me sad.
   *Saler.*           My wind, cooling my broth,
Would blow me to an ague when I thought
What harm a wind too great might do at sea.          25
I should not see the sandy hourglass run
But I should think of shallows and of flats,
And see my wealthy "Andrew" docked in sand,
Vailing her high top lower than her ribs
To kiss her burial. Should I go to church          30
And see the holy edifice of stone
And not bethink me straight of dangerous rocks,
Which, touching but my gentle vessel's side,
Would scatter all her spices on the stream,
Enrobe the roaring waters with my silks,          35
And, in a word, but even now worth this,
And now worth nothing? Shall I have the thought
To think on this, and shall I lack the thought
That such a thing bechanced would make me sad?
But tell not me! I know Antonio          40
Is sad to think upon his merchandise.
   *Ant.* Believe me, no. I thank my fortune for it,
My ventures are not in one bottom trusted,
Nor to one place; nor is my whole estate
Upon the fortune of this present year:          45
Therefore my merchandise makes me not sad.
   *Solan.* Why, then you are in love.
   *Ant.*                Fie, fie!
   *Solan.* Not in love neither? Then let us say you are sad
Because you are not merry; and 'twere as easy          50
For you to laugh, and leap, and say you are merry

"Two-headed Janus."
From Vincenzo Cartari,
*Imagini delli Dei de gl'Antichi* (1674).

52. **two-headed Janus**: the double-headed god of Roman mythology

55. **laugh . . . at a bagpiper**: laugh at something not funny. Only Scots find the drone of a bagpipe cheerful.

58. **Nestor**: the wisest of the Greek heroes in the Trojan War

70. **You grow exceeding strange**: you are getting to be strangers.

71. **We'll make our leisures to attend on yours**: we'll be available at your convenience.

77. **respect upon the world**: concern for worldly matters

Because you are not sad. Now, by two-headed Janus,
Nature hath framed strange fellows in her time:
Some that will evermore peep through their eyes,
And laugh like parrots at a bagpiper;                    55
And other of such vinegar aspect
That they'll not show their teeth in way of smile,
Though Nestor swear the jest be laughable.


Enter *Bassanio, Lorenzo,* and *Gratiano.*


Here comes Bassanio, your most noble kinsman,
Gratiano, and Lorenzo. Fare ye well.                     60
We leave you now with better company.
   *Saler.* I would have stayed till I had made you merry,
If worthier friends had not prevented me.
   *Ant.* Your worth is very dear in my regard.
I take it your own business calls on you,                65
And you embrace th' occasion to depart.
   *Saler.* Good morrow, my good lords.
   *Bass.* Good signiors both, when shall we laugh? Say,
      when?
You grow exceeding strange: must it be so?               70
   *Saler.* We'll make our leisures to attend on yours.
                         *Exeunt Salerio and Solanio.*
   *Lor.* My Lord Bassanio, since you have found Antonio,
We two will leave you, but at dinner time
I pray you have in mind where we must meet.
   *Bass.* I will not fail you.                          75
   *Gra.* You look not well, Signior Antonio,
You have too much respect upon the world:
They lose it that do buy it with much care.
Believe me, you are marvellously changed.

80. **hold:** regard

84. **old wrinkles:** abundant laugh lines; **old** was commonly used for emphasis.

86. **mortifying:** weakening. The Elizabethans believed that sorrowful sighing drained blood from the heart.

88. **alablaster:** alabaster; a stone often used for memorial busts of the dead

93. **Do cream and mantle:** acquire a sallow complexion from lack of vivacity, in the same way that scum dims the surface of a stagnant pond

94. **entertain:** maintain

95. **opinion:** reputation

96. **profound conceit:** depth of imaginative thought

97. **Sir Oracle:** the personification of prophetic wisdom

102-3. **dam those ears/ Which, hearing them, would call their brothers fools:** stop their ears against utterance that would earn the speakers the title "fool"

106. **gudgeon:** a small, easily caught fish used for bait. Gratiano compares reputation to something easily obtained and not worth having.

*Ant.* I hold the world but as the world, Gratiano,          80
A stage, where every man must play a part,
And mine a sad one.
    *Gra.*        Let me play the fool,
With mirth and laughter let old wrinkles come,
And let my liver rather heat with wine          85
Than my heart cool with mortifying groans.
Why should a man whose blood is warm within
Sit like his grandsire cut in alablaster?
Sleep when he wakes? and creep into the jaundice
By being peevish? I tell thee what, Antonio—          90
I love thee, and 'tis my love that speaks—
There are a sort of men whose visages
Do cream and mantle like a standing pond,
And do a wilful stillness entertain
With purpose to be dressed in an opinion          95
Of wisdom, gravity, profound conceit;
As who should say, "I am Sir Oracle,
And when I ope my lips, let no dog bark!"
O my Antonio, I do know of those
That therefore only are reputed wise          100
For saying nothing; when I am very sure,
If they should speak, would almost dam those ears
Which, hearing them, would call their brothers fools.
I'll tell thee more of this another time.
But fish not with this melancholy bait          105
For this fool gudgeon, this opinion.
Come, good Lorenzo. Fare ye well awhile.
I'll end my exhortation after dinner.
    *Lor.* Well, we will leave you then till dinner time.
I must be one of these same dumb wise men,          110
For Gratiano never lets me speak.

112. **mo**: more; see II. [vi.] 52.

114. **grow a talker for this gear**: grow garrulous on account of this nonsense (Gratiano's banter). Gear is an Elizabethan slang word with a variety of meanings from "stuff" to "business."

116. **neat's tongue**: calf's tongue

117. **Is that anything now**: now really, was there anything to that. Both the Quarto and Folio texts read, "It is that anything now." Nicholas Rowe emended the phrase to the reading we have given.

127. **disabled**: reduced

128. **something**: somewhat, to some degree; **swelling port**: magnificent style of living

130. **to be abridged**: at being curtailed

134. **gaged**: mortgaged

136. **warranty**: privilege

140-41. **if it stand . . ./ Within the eye of honor**: if it is honorable

143. **to your occasions**: for your necessities

*Gra.* Well, keep me company but two years mo,
Thou shalt not know the sound of thine own tongue.

*Ant.* Fare you well. I'll grow a talker for this gear.

*Gra.* Thanks, i' faith, for silence is only commendable  115
In a neat's tongue dried and a maid not vendible.

                    *Exeunt [Gratiano and Lorenzo].*

*Ant.* Is that anything now?

*Bass.* Gratiano speaks an infinite deal of nothing, more
than any man in all Venice. His reasons are as two grains
of wheat hid in two bushels of chaff: you shall seek all  120
day ere you find them, and when you have them, they
are not worth the search.

*Ant.* Well, tell me now, what lady is the same
To whom you swore a secret pilgrimage
That you today promised to tell me off?                  125

*Bass.* 'Tis not unknown to you, Antonio,
How much I have disabled mine estate
By something showing a more swelling port
Than my faint means would grant continuance;
Nor do I now make moan to be abridged                    130
From such a noble rate; but my chief care
Is to come fairly off from the great debts
Wherein my time, something too prodigal,
Hath left me gaged. To you, Antonio,
I owe the most in money and in love,                     135
And from your love I have a warranty
To unburden all my plots and purposes
How to get clear of all the debts I owe.

*Ant.* I pray you, good Bassanio, let me know it;
And if it stand, as you yourself still do,               140
Within the eye of honor, be assured
My purse, my person, my extremest means
Lie all unlocked to your occasions.

Jason, Medea, and the Golden Fleece.
From Ovid, *Metamorphoses* (1565).

146. **advised:** attentive

149. **what follows is pure innocence:** in Elizabethan usage "innocence" sometimes meant "folly." Bassanio is conscious that it may be foolish to ask a businessman to lend money to one already his debtor.

154. **or:** either

155. **hazard:** stake; that is, loan of money

156. **rest:** remain

158. **wind about my love with circumstance:** make a roundabout request instead of appealing directly to my friendship

160. **making question of my uttermost:** doubting the extent of my willingness to help you

165. **richly left:** well endowed by inheritance

175. **Colchos' strond:** the shore of Colchis, where Jason sought the Golden Fleece, in Greek mythology

*Bass.* In my schooldays, when I had lost one shaft,
I shot his fellow of the selfsame flight                    145
The selfsame way with more advised watch
To find the other forth; and by adventuring both
I oft found both. I urge this childhood proof
Because what follows is pure innocence.
I owe you much, and, like a wilful youth,                   150
That which I owe is lost; but if you please
To shoot another arrow that self way
Which you did shoot the first, I do not doubt,
As I will watch the aim, or to find both,
Or bring your latter hazard back again                      155
And thankfully rest debtor for the first.
    *Ant.* You know me well, and herein spend but time
To wind about my love with circumstance;
And out of doubt you do me now more wrong
In making question of my uttermost                          160
Than if you had made waste of all I have:
Then do but say to me what I should do
That in your knowledge may by me be done,
And I am pressed unto it: therefore speak.
    *Bass.* In Belmont is a lady richly left;                165
And she is fair, and, fairer than that word,
Of wondrous virtues—sometimes from her eyes
I did receive fair speechless messages—
Her name is Portia, nothing undervalued
To Cato's daughter, Brutus' Portia.                         170
Nor is the wide world ignorant of her worth,
For the four winds blow in from every coast
Renowned suitors, and her sunny locks
Hang on her temples like a golden fleece,
Which makes her seat of Belmont Colchos' strond,            175
And many Jasons come in quest of her.

179-80. **I have a mind presages me such thrift/ That I should questionless be fortunate**: I have a hunch that I will certainly be lucky enough to get rich.

182. **commodity**: property, i.e., collateral

188. **no question make/ To have it of my trust, or for my sake**: have no doubt that I shall get it either because of my good credit or for friendship

━━━━━━━━━━━━━━━━━━━━━━━━━━━━━━

**I. [ii.]** Portia and her attendant, Nerissa, discuss her unfortunate inability to choose her husband, and they analyze the quality of her wooers. Portia is bound by her father's wish that all suitors for her hand choose among three chests, of gold, silver, and lead, respectively. The man selecting the right chest may have her hand. Nerissa discloses that the suitors just discussed were unwilling to venture in accordance with the conditions and have departed; but a new suitor, the Prince of Morocco, is then announced.

━━━━━━━━━━━━━━━━━━━━━━

7. **to be seated in the mean**: to be of average status

7-8. **Superfluity comes sooner by white hairs**: excessive wealth ages the possessor more quickly; **competency**: compared with **superfluity**, "just enough"

9. **sentences**: *sententiae* (Latin), maxims

7

O my Antonio, had I but the means
To hold a rival place with one of them,
I have a mind presages me such thrift
That I should questionless be fortunate!                    180
 *Ant.* Thou know'st that all my fortunes are at sea,
Neither have I money, nor commodity
To raise a present sum. Therefore go forth;
Try what my credit can in Venice do.
That shall be racked, even to the uttermost,                185
To furnish thee to Belmont to fair Portia.
Go presently enquire, and so will I,
Where money is, and I no question make
To have it of my trust, or for my sake.

            *Exeunt.*

[Scene II. Portia's house at Belmont.]

Enter *Portia* with her waiting woman, *Nerissa.*

 *Por.* By my troth, Nerissa, my little body is aweary of
this great world.

 *Ner.* You would be, sweet madam, if your miseries
were in the same abundance as your good fortunes are;
and yet, for aught I see, they are as sick that surfeit with    5
too much as they that starve with nothing. It is no mean
happiness, therefore, to be seated in the mean. Superfluity
comes sooner by white hairs, but competency lives longer.

 *Por.* Good sentences, and well pronounced.

 *Ner.* They would be better if well followed.          10

 *Por.* If to do were as easy as to know what were good
to do, chapels had been churches, and poor men's cottages

Venetian ladies of quality at home.
From Vecellio, *De gli habiti antichi* (1590).

16. **blood**: passionate impulses
35. **level**: aim, guess
42. **County**: Count
44. **An**: if

princes' palaces. It is a good divine that follows his own
instructions. I can easier teach twenty what were good to
be done than be one of the twenty to follow mine own          15
teaching. The brain may devise laws for the blood, but a
hot temper leaps o'er a cold decree: such a hare is madness the youth, to skip o'er the meshes of good counsel
the cripple. But this reasoning is not in the fashion to
choose me a husband. O me, the word "choose"! I may      20
neither choose who I would nor refuse who I dislike, so
is the will of a living daughter curbed by the will of a
dead father. Is it not hard, Nerissa, that I cannot choose
one nor refuse none?

*Ner.* Your father was ever virtuous, and holy men at      25
their death have good inspirations: therefore the lott'ry
that he hath devised in these three chests of gold, silver,
and lead, whereof who chooses his meaning chooses you,
will no doubt never be chosen by any rightly but one who
you shall rightly love. But what warmth is there in your      30
affection towards any of these princely suitors that are already come?

*Por.* I pray thee overname them; and as thou namest
them, I will describe them; and according to my description level at my affection.                                    35

*Ner.* First, there is the Neapolitan prince.

*Por.* Ay, that's a colt indeed, for he doth nothing but
talk of his horse, and he makes it a great appropriation
unto his own good parts that he can shoe him himself: I
am much afeard my lady his mother played false with a      40
smith.

*Ner.* Then is there the County Palatine.

*Por.* He doth nothing but frown, as who should say,
"An you will not have me, choose!" He hears merry tales

45-6. **weeping philosopher**: Heraclitus of Ephesus, a philosopher who wept at the sight of humankind miserably struggling to accumulate money

50. **How say you by**: what do you say about

56. **throstle**: thrush; **straight**: at once; see I. [i.] 32.

57-8. **If I should marry him, I should marry twenty husbands**: his moods are so changeable that he would seem twenty men in one.

66. **proper**: handsome

67-8. **dumb show**: tableau without spoken dialogue

68. **suited**: dressed. There were many satires in this period on the English traveler's habit of adopting the fashions of foreign countries.

73-4. **borrowed a box of the ear of the Englishman, and swore he would pay him again when he was able**: received a blow from the Englishman without defending himself

and smiles not. I fear he will prove the weeping philoso-    45
pher when he grows old, being so full of unmannerly
sadness in his youth. I had rather be married to a death's-
head with a bone in his mouth than to either of these.
God defend me from these two!

*Ner.* How say you by the French lord, Monsieur Le    50
Bon?

*Por.* God made him, and therefore let him pass for a
man. In truth, I know it is a sin to be a mocker, but he—
why, he hath a horse better than the Neapolitan's, a better
bad habit of frowning than the Count Palatine. He is    55
every man in no man. If a throstle sing, he falls straight
a-cap'ring; he will fence with his own shadow. If I should
marry him, I should marry twenty husbands. If he would
despise me, I would forgive him; for if he love me to
madness, I shall never requite him.    60

*Ner.* What say you then to Falconbridge, the young
baron of England?

*Por.* You know I say nothing to him, for he understands
not me, nor I him. He hath neither Latin, French, nor
Italian; and you will come into the court and swear that I    65
have a poor pennyworth in the English. He is a proper
man's picture, but alas! who can converse with a dumb
show? How oddly he is suited! I think he bought his
doublet in Italy, his round hose in France, his bonnet in
Germany, and his behavior everywhere.    70

*Ner.* What think you of the Scottish lord, his neighbor?

*Por.* That he hath a neighborly charity in him, for he
borrowed a box of the ear of the Englishman, and swore
he would pay him again when he was able. I think the
Frenchman became his surety and sealed under for an-    75
other.

**77. German:** it was an Elizabethan convention to attribute drunkenness to all Germans.

**82-3. an the worst fall that ever fell:** if the worst that ever happened should happen; **make shift:** manage

**98. Sibylla:** the Cumaean Sibyl, the oracle of Apollo, to whom the god granted as many years of life as there were grains of sand in a handful she held; see Ovid, *Metamorphoses*, Book XIV.

**99. Diana:** the invincibly virgin goddess of Greek mythology

A German courtier.
From Jean de Glen,
*Des Habits, Moeurs, etc.* (1601).

The Cumaean Sibyl, "Sibylla."

*Ner.* How like you the young German, the Duke of
Saxony's nephew?

*Por.* Very vilely in the morning when he is sober, and
most vilely in the afternoon when he is drunk. When he    80
is best, he is a little worse than a man, and when he is
worst, he is little better than a beast: an the worst fall
that ever fell, I hope I shall make shift to go without him.

*Ner.* If he should offer to choose, and choose the right
casket, you should refuse to perform your father's will if    85
you should refuse to accept him.

*Por.* Therefore, for fear of the worst, I pray thee set a
deep glass of Rhenish wine on the contrary casket, for if
the devil be within and that temptation without, I know
he will choose it. I will do anything, Nerissa, ere I will be    90
married to a sponge.

*Ner.* You need not fear, lady, the having any of these
lords. They have acquainted me with their determina-
tions, which is indeed to return to their home, and to
trouble you with no more suit, unless you may be won by    95
some other sort than your father's imposition, depending
on the caskets.

*Por.* If I live to be as old as Sibylla, I will die as chaste
as Diana unless I be obtained by the manner of my
father's will. I am glad this parcel of wooers are so rea-    100
sonable, for there is not one among them but I dote on
his very absence; and I pray God grant them a fair departure.

*Ner.* Do you not remember, lady, in your father's time,
a Venetian, a scholar and a soldier, that came hither in    105
company of the Marquis of Montferrat?

*Por.* Yes, yes, it was Bassanio, as I think, so was he
called.

123. **shrive me:** give me absolution

〰〰〰〰〰〰〰〰〰〰〰〰〰〰〰〰〰〰〰〰〰〰〰

I. [iii.] Bassanio approaches the moneylender Shylock for a loan of 3,000 ducats for three months in Antonio's name. Shylock reflects that Antonio's credit is good, although his cash is dependent on the ships he has trading abroad. Aside, however, he declares his hatred of Antonio, who will not lend money at interest and has interfered with Shylock's own profits, and who also has treated Shylock with contempt because he is a Jew. Nevertheless, he agrees to lend the sum requested if Antonio will sign a bond to forfeit a pound of his own flesh if the loan is not repaid on the stipulated day. Bassanio dislikes the terms and distrusts Shylock, but Antonio assures him that his ships will return a month before the money is due.

〰〰〰〰〰〰〰〰〰〰〰〰〰〰〰〰〰

1. **ducats:** the Venetian gold ducat was probably worth between $6.50 and $7.00 in modern purchasing power. Bassanio is thus asking for the sum of approximately $20,000 in the currency of today.

*Ner.* True, madam. He, of all the men that ever my foolish eyes looked upon, was the best deserving a fair 110 lady.

*Por.* I remember him well, and I remember him worthy of thy praise.

Enter a *Servingman.*

How now? What news?

*Serv.* The four strangers seek for you, madam, to take 115 their leave; and there is a forerunner come from a fifth, the Prince of Morocco, who brings word the Prince his master will be here tonight.

*Por.* If I could bid the fifth welcome with so good heart as I can bid the other four farewell, I should be 120 glad of his approach. If he have the condition of a saint and the complexion of a devil, I had rather he should shrive me than wive me.

Come, Nerissa. Sirrah, go before.

Whiles we shut the gate upon one wooer, another knocks 125 at the door.

*Exeunt.*

[Scene III. A street in Venice.]

Enter *Bassanio* with *Shylock the Jew.*

*Shy.* Three thousand ducats—well.
*Bass.* Ay, sir, for three months.
*Shy.* For three months—well.

The Rialto Bridge.

7. **May you stead me:** can you help me.

15-6. **he is sufficient:** he is able to pay; **in supposition:** in expectation

18. **the Rialto:** the Wall Street of Venice

*Bass.* For the which, as I told you, Antonio shall be bound.                                                                          5

*Shy.* Antonio shall become bound—well.

*Bass.* May you stead me? Will you pleasure me? Shall I know your answer?

*Shy.* Three thousand ducats for three months, and Antonio bound.                                                                 10

*Bass.* Your answer to that.

*Shy.* Antonio is a good man.

*Bass.* Have you heard any imputation to the contrary?

*Shy.* Ho, no, no, no, no! My meaning in saying he is a good man is to have you understand me that he is suf-    15
ficient. Yet his means are in supposition: he hath an argosy bound to Tripolis, another to the Indies. I understand, moreover, upon the Rialto, he hath a third at Mexico, a fourth for England, and other ventures he hath,
squand'red abroad. But ships are but boards, sailors but    20
men; there be land rats and water rats, water thieves and land thieves—I mean pirates; and then there is the peril
of waters, winds, and rocks—the man is, notwithstand-
ing, sufficient—three thousand ducats—I think I may take his bond.                                                                       25

*Bass.* Be assured you may.

*Shy.* I will be assured I may; and that I may be assured, I will bethink me. May I speak with Antonio?

*Bass.* If it please you to dine with us.

*Shy.* Yes, to smell pork, to eat of the habitation which    30
your prophet the Nazarite conjured the devil into! I will buy with you, sell with you, talk with you, walk with
you, and so following; but I will not eat with you, drink with you, nor pray with you. What news on the Rialto?
Who is he comes here?                                                                      35

37. **publican**: innkeeper. Shylock is contemptuous of Antonio's goodhearted kindness, which to him indicates a soft desire to be popular.

41. usance: interest on loans

42. upon the hip: at my mercy; a wrestling term

45. Even there: that is, on the Rialto

46. thrift: wealth; see I. [i.] 179.

55. soft: hold on

56. Rest you fair: good luck to you.

60. ripe: urgent

61. Is he yet possessed: does he know

Enter *Antonio*.

*Bass.* This is Signior Antonio.

*Shy.* [*Aside*] How like a fawning publican he looks!
I hate him for he is a Christian;
But more for that in low simplicity
He lends out money gratis and brings down          40
The rate of usance here with us in Venice.
If I can catch him once upon the hip,
I will feed fat the ancient grudge I bear him.
He hates our sacred nation, and he rails,
Even there where merchants most do congregate,     45
On me, my bargains, and my well-won thrift,
Which he calls interest. Cursed be my tribe
If I forgive him!

*Bass.*          Shylock, do you hear?

*Shy.* I am debating of my present store,          50
And by the near guess of my memory
I cannot instantly raise up the gross
Of full three thousand ducats. What of that?
Tubal, a wealthy Hebrew of my tribe,
Will furnish me. But soft! How many months         55
Do you desire?—[*To Antonio*] Rest you fair, good signior!
Your worship was the last man in our mouths.

*Ant.* Shylock, albeit I neither lend nor borrow
By taking nor by giving of excess,
Yet, to supply the ripe wants of my friend,        60
I'll break a custom. [*To Bassanio*] Is he yet possessed
How much ye would?

*Shy.*               Ay, ay, three thousand ducats.

*Ant.* And for three months.

67. **Methoughts:** methought; Shakespeare uses this form on several occasions.

70. **Jacob:** Shylock refers to the story of Jacob and Laban in Genesis 30:31-43.

77. **were compromised:** had come to terms

78. **eanlings:** new-born lambs; **pied:** spotted

83. **pilled me:** peeled. The shepherd, of course, did not peel the twigs for Shylock; "me" may be used here merely to add an extra syllable.

86. **eaning time:** lambing time

87. **Fall:** drop

90. **venture:** speculation

93. **Was this inserted to make interest good:** did you relate this scriptural incident to justify interest.

*Shy.* I had forgot—three months, you told me so.　　65
Well then, your bond. And let me see—but hear you:
Methoughts you said you neither lend nor borrow
Upon advantage.

*Ant.*　　　　I do never use it.

*Shy.* When Jacob grazed his uncle Laban's sheep—　　70
This Jacob from our holy Abram was
(As his wise mother wrought in his behalf)
The third possessor; ay, he was the third—

*Ant.* And what of him? Did he take interest?

*Shy.* No, not take interest; not, as you would say,　　75
Directly int'rest. Mark what Jacob did.
When Laban and himself were compromised
That all the eanlings which were streaked and pied
Should fall as Jacob's hire, the ewes, being rank,
In end of autumn turned to the rams,　　80
And when the work of generation was
Between these woolly breeders in the act,
The skilful shepherd pilled me certain wands,
And, in the doing of the deed of kind,
He stuck them up before the fulsome ewes,　　85
Who then conceiving, did in eaning time
Fall parti-colored lambs, and those were Jacob's.
This was a way to thrive, and he was blest;
And thrift is blessing, if men steal it not.

*Ant.* This was a venture, sir, that Jacob served for,　　90
A thing not in his power to bring to pass,
But swayed and fashioned by the hand of heaven.
Was this inserted to make interest good?
Or is your gold and silver ewes and rams?

*Shy.* I cannot tell, I make it breed as fast—　　95
But note me, signior.

107. **rated:** berated, reviled

108. **moneys:** sums of money, a common plural

112. **spet:** spat; **gaberdine:** a loose garment such as a cloak or mantle

113. **use:** "lending at interest" as well as "using"

115. **Go to then:** good enough; a vague interjection

117. **void your rheum:** spit

   *Ant.* [*Aside*]     Mark you this, Bassanio,
The devil can cite Scripture for his purpose.
An evil soul, producing holy witness,
Is like a villain with a smiling cheek,          100
A goodly apple rotten at the heart.
O, what a goodly outside falsehood hath!
   *Shy.* Three thousand ducats—'tis a good round sum.
Three months from twelve—then, let me see, the rate—
   *Ant.* Well, Shylock, shall we be beholding to you?   105
   *Shy.* Signior Antonio, many a time and oft
In the Rialto you have rated me
About my moneys and my usances:
Still have I borne it with a patient shrug,
For suff'rance is the badge of all our tribe.     110
You call me misbeliever, cutthroat dog,
And spet upon my Jewish gaberdine,
And all for use of that which is mine own.
Well then, it now appears you need my help:
Go to then, you come to me and you say,    115
"Shylock, we would have moneys." You say so—
You that did void your rheum upon my beard
And foot me as you spurn a stranger cur
Over your threshold. Moneys is your suit.
What should I say to you? Should I not say,   120
"Hath a dog money? Is it possible
A cur can lend three thousand ducats?" or
Shall I bend low, and in a bondman's key,
With bated breath and whisp'ring humbleness,
Say this:                     125
"Fair sir, you spet on me on Wednesday last;
You spurned me such a day; another time
You called me dog; and for these courtesies
I'll lend you thus much moneys"?

134. **A breed for barren metal:** interest as the unnatural offspring of gold and silver

141. **doit:** jot, from a small coin once used by the Dutch

144. **This were kindness:** that is, this would be kindness (if done as described).

147. **single:** mere; that is, a bond signed by Antonio without security or cosigners; **in a merry sport:** just for fun. Shylock makes a pretense that the forfeit will not be taken seriously.

151. **equal:** exact

154. **Content:** I am agreed.

*Ant.* I am as like to call thee so again,  130
To spet on thee again, to spurn thee too.
If thou wilt lend this money, lend it not
As to thy friends, for when did friendship take
A breed for barren metal of his friend?
But lend it rather to thine enemy,  135
Who if he break, thou mayst with better face
Exact the penalty.

 *Shy.*    Why, look you, how you storm!
I would be friends with you and have your love,
Forget the shames that you have stained me with,  140
Supply your present wants, and take no doit
Of usance for my moneys,
And you'll not hear me. This is kind I offer.

 *Bass.* This were kindness.

 *Shy.*    This kindness will I show.  145
Go with me to a notary, seal me there
Your single bond; and, in a merry sport,
If you repay me not on such a day,
In such a place, such sum or sums as are
Expressed in the condition, let the forfeit  150
Be nominated for an equal pound
Of your fair flesh, to be cut off and taken
In what part of your body pleaseth me.

 *Ant.* Content, in faith. I'll seal to such a bond,
And say there is much kindness in the Jew.  155

 *Bass.* You shall not seal to such a bond for me!
I'll rather dwell in my necessity.

 *Ant.* Why, fear not, man! I will not forfeit it.
Within these two months—that's a month before
This bond expires—I do expect return  160
Of thrice three times the value of this bond.

171. **so:** well and good; fine

177. **fearful:** to be feared; untrustworthy

180. **Hie thee:** hurry; **gentle Jew:** a pun on "gentile;" see also other such quibbles at II. [iv.] 37 and II. [vi.] 53.

182. **I like not fair terms and a villain's mind:** I distrust what appear fair terms when they are offered by a villain.

*Shy.* O father Abram, what these Christians are,
Whose own hard dealing teaches them suspect
The thoughts of others! Pray you tell me this:
If he should break his day, what should I gain          165
By the exaction of the forfeiture?
A pound of man's flesh taken from a man
Is not so estimable, profitable neither,
As flesh of muttons, beefs, or goats. I say,
To buy his favor I extend this friendship.              170
If he will take it, so; if not, adieu;
And for my love I pray you wrong me not.
      *Ant.* Yes, Shylock, I will seal unto this bond.
      *Shy.* Then meet me forthwith at the notary's;
Give him direction for this merry bond,                 175
And I will go and purse the ducats straight,
See to my house, left in the fearful guard
Of an unthrifty knave, and presently
I will be with you.
      *Ant.*              Hie thee, gentle Jew.          180
                              *Exit* [*Shylock*].
The Hebrew will turn Christian; he grows kind.
      *Bass.* I like not fair terms and a villain's mind.
      *Ant.* Come on, in this there can be no dismay;
My ships come home a month before the day.

                              *Exeunt.*

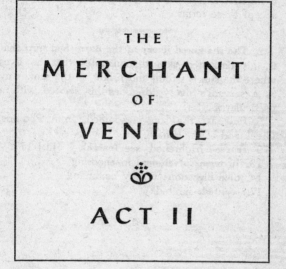

# THE
# MERCHANT
## OF
# VENICE

## ACT II

**II.** [i.] The Prince of Morocco arrives at Portia's estate to try for her hand. Portia tells him he must stand or fall on the verdict of the caskets and he must swear never to seek another woman for a wife if he should lose. Morocco expresses willingness to accept these terms.

 ┄┄┄┄┄┄┄┄┄┄┄┄┄┄┄

2. **The shadowed livery of the burnished sun:** that is, his darkened skin demonstrates that he lives where the sun is strong and bright, in the same way as a servant's livery identifies his service with a particular master.

5. **Phœbus:** the sun personified, from Phœbus, Greek god of the sun

9. **feared:** frightened; see **fearful,** I. [iii.] 177.

13. **In terms of choice:** in choosing

14. **nice direction:** finicky command

17. **scanted:** limited

# ACT II

[Scene I. Portia's house at Belmont.]

*Flourish cornets.* Enter [the *Prince of*] *Morocco*, a tawny
Moor, all in white, and three of four *Followers* accordingly, with *Portia*, *Nerissa*, and their *Train*.

*Mor.* Mislike me not for my complexion,
The shadowed livery of the burnished sun,
To whom I am a neighbor and near bred.
Bring me the fairest creature northward born,
Where Phœbus' fire scarce thaws the icicles,                    5
And let us make incision for your love
To prove whose blood is reddest, his or mine.
I tell thee, lady, this aspect of mine
Hath feared the valiant—by my love I swear,
The best-regarded virgins of our clime                          10
Have loved it too—I would not change this hue,
Except to steal your thoughts, my gentle queen.
*Por.* In terms of choice I am not solely led
By nice direction of a maiden's eyes:
Besides, the lott'ry of my destiny                              15
Bars me the right of voluntary choosing.
But, if my father had not scanted me,

18

20. **stood:** would stand

26. **the Sophy:** the King of Persia

27. **Sultan Solyman:** Solyman the Magnificent of Turkey

31. **'a:** he

33. **Hercules:** celebrated strong man in classical mythology; **Lichas:** Hercules' attendant; see Ovid, *Metamorphoses*, Book IX.

36. **Alcides:** another name for Hercules; **page:** a correction suggested by Alexander Pope where the Quarto and Folio texts have "rage"

Solyman the Magnificent.

44. **be advised:** take careful thought before acting.

Hercules and Lichas.
From Ovid, *Metamorphoseon* (1565).

And hedged me by his wit to yield myself
His wife who wins me by that means I told you,
Yourself, renowned Prince, then stood as fair          20
As any comer I have looked on yet
For my affection.

 *Mor.*   Even for that I thank you.
Therefore I pray you lead me to the caskets
To try my fortune. By this scimitar,                   25
That slew the Sophy and a Persian prince
That won three fields of Sultan Solyman,
I would o'erstare the sternest eyes that look,
Outbrave the heart most daring on the earth,
Pluck the young sucking cubs from the she-bear,        30
Yea, mock the lion when 'a roars for prey,
To win thee, lady. But, alas the while!
If Hercules and Lichas play at dice
Which is the better man, the greater throw
May turn by fortune from the weaker hand:              35
So is Alcides beaten by his page,
And so may I, blind Fortune leading me,
Miss that which one unworthier may attain,
And die with grieving.

 *Por.*   You must take your chance,   40
And either not attempt to choose at all,
Or swear before you choose, if you choose wrong,
Never to speak to lady afterward
In way of marriage. Therefore be advised.

 *Mor.* Nor will not. Come, bring me unto my chance.   45

 *Por.* First, forward to the temple; after dinner
Your hazard shall be made.

 *Mor.*   Good fortune then!
To make me blest or cursed'st among men.

        *Exeunt.*

**II. [ii.]** Launcelot Gobbo, a servant of Shylock, debates with himself in humorous terms whether to seek a new employer. His father appears in search of him and Launcelot teases him a bit before revealing his identity to the nearly blind old man. When Bassanio enters, Launcelot, with his father's help, solicits a place in his service, and Bassanio agrees to employ him.

Bassanio's friend Gratiano enters and begs to accompany him to Belmont. Bassanio assents on condition that he behave with more decorum than he shows at home among friends.

<hr/>

9. **"Via"**: away; an Italian word used in England to urge horses forward

12. **hanging about the neck of my heart**: that is, clinging, woman-fashion, and weakening his courage

15. **did something smack**: was somewhat inclined (to dishonesty)

21. **God bless the mark**: an exclamation to ward off bad luck before mentioning something unpleasant or dangerous

23. **saving your reverence**: a prefatory phrase used to apologize for a comment that might be offensive

24. **incarnation**: incarnate; in the flesh

25. **in my conscience**: as I really see it

[Scene II. A street in Venice.]

Enter [*Launcelot*] *the Clown,* alone.

*Laun.* Certainly my conscience will serve me to run from this Jew my master. The fiend is at mine elbow and tempts me, saying to me, "Gobbo, Launcelot Gobbo, good Launcelot," or "good Gobbo," or "good Launcelot Gobbo, use your legs, take the start, run away." My conscience says, "No. Take heed, honest Launcelot; take heed, honest Gobbo," or, as aforesaid, "honest Launcelot Gobbo, do not run; scorn running with thy heels." Well, the most courageous fiend bids me pack. "Via!" says the fiend. "Away!" says the fiend. "For the heavens, rouse up a brave mind," says the fiend, "and run." Well, my conscience, hanging about the neck of my heart, says very wisely to me, "My honest friend Launcelot, being an honest man's son"—or rather an honest woman's son, for indeed my father did something smack, something grow to, he had a kind of taste—Well, my conscience says, "Launcelot, budge not." "Budge," says the fiend. "Budge not," says my conscience. "Conscience," say I, "you counsel well." "Fiend," say I, "you counsel well." To be ruled by my conscience, I should stay with the Jew my master, who (God bless the mark!) is a kind of devil; and, to run away from the Jew, I should be ruled by the fiend, who (saving your reverence) is the devil himself. Certainly the Jew is the very devil incarnation, and, in my conscience, my conscience is but a kind of hard conscience to offer to counsel me to stay with the Jew. The fiend gives the more friendly counsel. I will run, fiend; my heels are at your commandment; I will run.

32-3. **sand-blind**: a corruption of the Anglo-Saxon *samblind*, half-blind; **high-gravel-blind**: Launcelot coins a word for a degree of blindness between "sand" (half) and "stone" (totally).

37. **marry**: an exclamation, originally an oath derived from the name of the Virgin Mary

40. **Be God's sonties**: by God's holiness; **sonties** is probably a corruption of Old French *saintee*.

44. **raise the waters**: provoke his tears

48. **well to live**: likely to live long

52. **ergo**: the Latin for "therefore," a common phrase in formal logic. Shakespeare has his clowns use it for comic effect in *All's Well That Ends Well* and *The Comedy of Errors*, as well as here.

57-8. **the Sisters Three**: another name for the three Fates of Greek mythology

Enter *Old Gobbo*, with a basket.

*Gob.* Master young man, you, I pray you, which is
the way to Master Jew's?                                            30
*Laun.* [*Aside*] O heavens, this is my true-begotten
father! who, being more than sand-blind, high-gravel-
blind, knows me not. I will try confusions with him.
*Gob.* Master young gentleman, I pray you which is the
way to Master Jew's?                                               35
*Laun.* Turn up on your right hand at the next turning,
but, at the next turning of all, on your left; marry, at the
very next turning, turn of no hand, but turn down indi-
rectly to the Jew's house.
*Gob.* Be God's sonties, 'twill be a hard way to hit!       40
Can you tell me whether one Launcelot that dwells with
him, dwell with him or no?
*Laun.* Talk you of young Master Launcelot? [*Aside*]
Mark me now! Now will I raise the waters.—Talk you of
young Master Launcelot?                                            45
*Gob.* No master, sir, but a poor man's son. His father,
though I say't, is an honest exceeding poor man, and,
God be thanked, well to live.
*Laun.* Well, let his father be what 'a will, we talk of
young Master Launcelot.                                            50
*Gob.* Your worship's friend, and Launcelot, sir.
*Laun.* But, I pray you, ergo, old man, ergo, I beseech
you, talk you of young Master Launcelot?
*Gob.* Of Launcelot, an't please your mastership.
*Laun.* Ergo Master Launcelot. Talk not of Master        55
Launcelot, father; for the young gentleman, according to
Fates and Destinies and such odd sayings, the Sisters

The Three Fates.
From Vincenzo Cartari,
*Imagini delli Dei de gl'Antichi* (1674).

**86-7. Lord worshipped might he be: God be praised; what a beard hast thou got:** stage tradition has Launcelot kneel facing away from his father, who pats the back of his head and mistakes it for a beard.

**88. fill-horse:** a horse that draws between shafts (fills)

22

Three and such branches of learning, is indeed deceased,
or, as you would say in plain terms, gone to heaven.

*Gob.* Marry, God forbid! The boy was the very staff    60
of my age, my very prop.

*Laun.* [*Aside*] Do I look like a cudgel or a hovel-post,
a staff, or a prop?—Do you know me, father?

*Gob.* Alack the day, I know you not, young gentleman! but I pray you tell me, is my boy (God rest his    65
soul!) alive or dead?

*Laun.* Do you not know me, father?

*Gob.* Alack, sir, I am sand-blind! I know you not.

*Laun.* Nay, indeed, if you had your eyes, you might
fail of the knowing me. It is a wise father that knows his    70
own child. Well, old man, I will tell you news of your
son. [*Kneels.*] Give me your blessing. Truth will come to
light; murder cannot be hid long—a man's son may, but
in the end truth will out.

*Gob.* Pray you, sir, stand up. I am sure you are not    75
Launcelot, my boy.

*Laun.* Pray you, let's have no more fooling about it,
but give me your blessing. I am Launcelot—your boy that
was, your son that is, your child that shall be.

*Gob.* I cannot think you are my son.    80

*Laun.* I know not what I shall think of that; but I am
Launcelot, the Jew's man, and I am sure Margery your
wife is my mother.

*Gob.* Her name is Margery indeed. I'll be sworn, if
thou be Launcelot, thou art mine own flesh and blood.    85
Lord worshipped might he be, what a beard hast thou
got! Thou hast got more hair on thy chin than Dobbin
my fill-horse has on his tail.

*Laun.* [*Rises.*] It should seem then that Dobbin's tail

Old Gobbo (a sixteenth-century Italian rustic).
From Vecellio, *De gli habiti antichi* (1590).

96. **set up my rest**: determined to stake all; a term from primero, a game of chance

97. **a very Jew**: unqualifiedly a Jew

98. **halter**: hangman's noose

99. **tell**: count

100. **Give me**: give for me

111. **Gramercy**: a corruption of the French *grant merci;* that is, many thanks

115. **infection**: affection, inclination

grows backward. I am sure he had more hair of his tail   90
than I have of my face when I last saw him.

*Gob.* Lord, how art thou changed! How dost thou and
thy master agree? I have brought him a present. How
'gree you now?

*Laun.* Well, well, but, for mine own part, as I have   95
set up my rest to run away, so I will not rest till I have
run some ground. My master's a very Jew. Give him a
present? Give him a halter! I am famished in his service.
You may tell every finger I have with my ribs. Father, I
am glad you are come. Give me your present to one Mas-   100
ter Bassanio, who indeed gives rare new liveries. If I
serve not him, I will run as far as God has any ground.
O rare fortune! here comes the man. To him, father, for
I am a Jew if I serve the Jew any longer.

Enter *Bassanio*, with [*Leonardo* and] a *Follower*
or two.

*Bass.* You may do so, but let it be so hasted that sup-   105
per be ready at the farthest by five of the clock. See
these letters delivered, put the liveries to making, and
desire Gratiano to come anon to my lodging.

*Exit one of his men.*

*Laun.* To him, father.

*Gob.* God bless your worship!   110

*Bass.* Gramercy. Wouldst thou aught with me?

*Gob.* Here's my son, sir, a poor boy—

*Laun.* Not a poor boy, sir, but the rich Jew's man,
that would, sir, as my father shall specify—

*Gob.* He hath a great infection, sir, as one would say,   115
to serve—

120. **scarce cater-cousins**: not even distantly related; that is, not on close terms

123. **frutify**: Launcelot means something like "notify" but his vocabulary is not equal to his desire to use fine language.

126. **impertinent**: "pertinent" or "appurtenant"

132. **defect**: another error, probably for "effect"

135. **preferred thee**: recommended you

138. **The old proverb**: "The grace of God is enough."

144. **guarded**: trimmed with braid

147. **table**: palm of the hand, specifically that part which is used for fortunetelling

*Laun.* Indeed, the short and the long is, I serve the
Jew, and have a desire, as my father shall specify—

*Gob.* His master and he (saving your worship's reverence) are scarce cater-cousins.                           120

*Laun.* To be brief, the very truth is, that the Jew having done me wrong, doth cause me, as my father, being,
I hope, an old man, shall frutify unto you—

*Gob.* I have here a dish of doves that I would bestow
upon your worship; and my suit is—                        125

*Laun.* In very brief, the suit is impertinent to myself,
as your worship shall know by this honest old man; and,
though I say it, though old man, yet poor man, my
father.

*Bass.* One speak for both. What would you?            130
*Laun.* Serve you, sir.
*Gob.* That is the very defect of the matter, sir.
*Bass.* I know thee well; thou hast obtained thy suit.
Shylock thy master spoke with me this day
And hath preferred thee, if it be preferment             135
To leave a rich Jew's service to become
The follower of so poor a gentleman.

*Laun.* The old proverb is very well parted between
my master Shylock and you, sir: you have the grace of
God, sir, and he hath enough.                             140

*Bass.* Thou speak'st it well. Go, father, with thy son.
Take leave of thy old master and enquire
My lodging out. [*To a Servant*] Give him a livery
More guarded than his fellows'. See it done.

*Laun.* Father, in. I cannot get a service, no! I have  145
ne'er a tongue in my head! Well, [*studying his palm*] if
any man in Italy have a fairer table which doth offer to
swear upon a book—! I shall have good fortune. Go to,
here's a simple line of life! Here's a small trifle of wives!

Fortune personified.
From Vincenzo Cartari,
*Imagini delli Dei de gl'Antichi* (1674).

150. **a 'leven:** eleven, a common form in colloquial speech of the time

151. **coming-in:** income

152-53. **to be in peril of my life with the edge of
a feather-bed:** a colloquial expression about the
danger of marriage

154. **gear:** stuff; see I. [i.] 114. Launcelot refers
to the fortune he has just read in his hand, which
he considers tolerably good.

172. **Parts:** characteristics

174-75. **show/ Something too liberal:** appear
somewhat too unreserved

176. **allay:** moderate

178. **misconst'red:** misconstrued, misjudged

25

Alas, fifteen wives is nothing! a 'leven widows and nine 150
maids is a simple coming-in for one man; and then to
scape drowning thrice, and to be in peril of my life with
the edge of a feather-bed! Here are simple scapes. Well,
if Fortune be a woman, she's a good wench for this gear.
Father, come. I'll take my leave of the Jew in the twin- 155
kling.                              *Exit [with Old Gobbo].*
    *Bass.* I pray thee, good Leonardo, think on this:
These things being bought and orderly bestowed,
Return in haste, for I do feast tonight
My best-esteemed acquaintance. Hie thee, go.        160
    *Leon.* My best endeavors shall be done herein.


Enter *Gratiano.*


    *Gra.* Where's your master?
    *Leon.*                              Yonder, sir, he walks. *Exit.*
    *Gra.* Signior Bassanio!
    *Bass.* Gratiano!                                    165
    *Gra.* I have a suit to you.
    *Bass.*                      You have obtained it.
    *Gra.* You must not deny me, I must go with you
To Belmont.
    *Bass.* Why, then you must. But hear thee, Gratiano. 170
Thou art too wild, too rude, and bold of voice—
Parts that become thee happily enough
And in such eyes as ours appear not faults;
But where thou art not known, why, there they show
Something too liberal. Pray thee take pain          175
To allay with some cold drops of modesty
Thy skipping spirit, lest through thy wild behavior
I be misconst'red in the place I go to
And lose my hopes.

181. **put on a sober habit:** clothe himself in a pretense of gravity

186. **Use all the observance of civility:** mind my manners

187. **well studied in a sad ostent:** accustomed to giving the appearance of sober thoughtfulness

192. **were pity:** would be a pity

IIIIIIIIIIIIIIIIIIIIIIIIIIIIIIIIIIIIIIIIIIIIIIIIIIIIIIIIIIII

**II. [iii.]** Jessica, Shylock's daughter, says good-by to Launcelot with some regret but sends a letter by him to Lorenzo, who dines at Bassanio's that night. When Launcelot has left, she indicates that she and her father are alike only in blood and that she hopes to marry Lorenzo.

*Gra.*              Signior Bassanio, hear me:            180
If I do not put on a sober habit,
Talk with respect, and swear but now and then,
Wear prayer books in my pocket, look demurely,
Nay more, while grace is saying hood mine eyes
Thus with my hat, and sigh, and say amen,             185
Use all the observance of civility
Like one well studied in a sad ostent
To please his grandam, never trust me more.
    *Bass.* Well, we shall see your bearing.
    *Gra.* Nay, but I bar tonight; you shall not gauge me 190
By what we do tonight.
    *Bass.*              No, that were pity.
I would entreat you rather to put on
Your boldest suit of mirth, for we have friends
That purpose merriment: but fare you well,            195
I have some business.
    *Gra.* And I must to Lorenzo and the rest;
But we will visit you at supper time.

                                        *Exeunt.*

[Scene III. Shylock's house in Venice.]

Enter *Jessica* and [*Launcelot*] *the Clown.*

*Jes.* I am sorry thou wilt leave my father so.
Our house is hell, and thou, a merry devil,
Didst rob it of some taste of tediousness;
But fare thee well, there is a ducat for thee;
And, Launcelot, soon at supper shalt thou see             5
Lorenzo, who is thy new master's guest.

10. **exhibit**: Launcelot's mistake for "inhibit" or "prohibit"

<hr />

**II. [iv.]** Gratiano, Lorenzo, and two other friends of Bassanio are discussing plans for a masque when Launcelot enters with Jessica's letter informing Lorenzo of her plans to elope with him that night disguised as a page.

<hr />

6. **quaintly ordered**: skilfully managed
9. **furnish us**: make our preparations

Give him this letter—do it secretly—
And so farewell: I would not have my father
See me in talk with thee.

   *Laun.* Adieu! tears exhibit my tongue, most beautiful   10
pagan, most sweet Jew! if a Christian did not play the
knave and get thee, I am much deceived. But adieu!
these foolish drops do something drown my manly spirit:
adieu!

   *Jes.* Farewell, good Launcelot.   15

                                    *Exit [Launcelot].*

Alack, what heinous sin is it in me
To be ashamed to be my father's child!
But though I am a daughter to his blood,
I am not to his manners. O Lorenzo,
If thou keep promise, I shall end this strife,   20
Become a Christian and thy loving wife.

                                            *Exit.*

[Scene IV. A street in Venice.]

Enter *Gratiano, Lorenzo, Salerio,* and *Solanio.*

   *Lor.* Nay, we will slink away in supper time,
Disguise us at my lodging, and return
All in an hour.

   *Gra.* We have not made good preparation.

   *Saler.* We have not spoke us yet of torchbearers.   5

   *Solan.* 'Tis vile, unless it may be quaintly ordered,
And better in my mind not undertook.

   *Lor.* 'Tis now but four o'clock; we have two hours
To furnish us.

11-2. **break up:** open; **it shall seem to signify:** it will inform you. The clown uses a wordy phrase which was common in courtly Elizabethan speech.

17. **By your leave, sir:** a polite request to be dismissed

24. **masque:** a dramatic entertainment of music, dance, and pantomime

29. **some hour hence:** in about an hour

37. **gentle:** see I. [iii.] 180 for the same pun on "gentle-Gentile."

*Enter Launcelot, with a letter.*

Friend Launcelot, what's the news?          10

*Laun.* An it shall please you to break up this, it shall
seem to signify.

*Lor.* I know the hand. In faith, 'tis a fair hand,
And whiter than the paper it writ on
Is the fair hand that writ.          15

*Gra.*                  Love-news, in faith!

*Laun.* By your leave, sir.

*Lor.* Whither goest thou?

*Laun.* Marry, sir, to bid my old master the Jew to sup
tonight with my new master the Christian.          20

*Lor.* Hold here, take this. Tell gentle Jessica
I will not fail her. Speak it privately.

*[Exit Launcelot.]*

Go, gentlemen,
Will you prepare you for this masque tonight?
I am provided of a torchbearer.          25

*Saler.* Ay, marry, I'll be gone about it straight.

*Solan.* And so will I.

*Lor.*                  Meet me and Gratiano
At Gratiano's lodging some hour hence.

*Saler.* 'Tis good we do so.          30

*Exeunt [Salerio and Solanio].*

*Gra.* Was not that letter from fair Jessica?

*Lor.* I must needs tell thee all. She hath directed
How I shall take her from her father's house;
What gold and jewels she is furnished with;
What page's suit she hath in readiness.          35
If e'er the Jew her father come to heaven,
It will be for his gentle daughter's sake;

**II.** [v.] Launcelot invites Shylock to Bassanio's to dinner and Shylock accepts with many misgivings and warnings to Jessica to guard the house well. Launcelot manages to convey a message to Jessica indicating that Lorenzo has received her letter and she may expect him that night.

And never dare misfortune cross her foot,
Unless she do it under this excuse,
That she is issue to a faithless Jew.                        40
Come, go with me; peruse this as thou goest.
Fair Jessica shall be my torchbearer.

*Exeunt.*

[Scene V. Before Shylock's house in Venice.]

Enter [*the*] *Jew* [*Shylock*] and his man [*Launcelot*]
that was the *Clown.*

*Shy.* Well, thou shalt see, thy eyes shall be thy judge,
The difference of old Shylock and Bassanio.—
What, Jessica!—Thou shalt not gormandize
As thou hast done with me—What, Jessica!—
And sleep, and snore, and rend apparel out.—            5
Why, Jessica, I say!
    *Laun.*            Why, Jessica!
*Shy.* Who bids thee call? I do not bid thee call.
*Laun.* Your worship was wont to tell me I could do
nothing without bidding.                                    10

Enter *Jessica.*

*Jes.* Call you? What is your will?
*Shy.* I am bid forth to supper, Jessica.
There are my keys: but wherefore should I go?
I am not bid for love; they flatter me.
But yet I'll go in hate, to feed upon                       15

21. **reproach:** approach; another of Launcelot's garblings, which Shylock answers literally

25. **my nose fell a-bleeding:** a nosebleed was commonly considered a bad omen.

27. **Ash Wednesday was four year:** four years ago last Ash Wednesday. The whole passage is a deliberate mockery of typical contemporary fortunetelling jargon.

30. **wry-necked fife:** that is, the fife player, referring to the angle at which a fife is held

33. **varnished:** 1) wearing varnished masks, 2) artificially improved. Shylock probably intends a sneer at the hypocrisy of most Christians.

35. **fopp'ry:** foolishness

36. **Jacob's staff:** Shylock appropriately swears by one of the patriarchs of the Old Testament; see Genesis 32:10.

43. **Jew's:** spelled "Jewes" in the early texts and pronounced as two syllables

44. **Hagar's offspring:** a term of contempt, meaning "outcast"

46. **patch:** fool

The prodigal Christian. Jessica, my girl,
Look to my house. I am right loath to go—
There is some ill a-brewing towards my rest,
For I did dream of money bags tonight.

*Laun.* I beseech you, sir, go. My young master doth    20
expect your reproach.

*Shy.* So do I his.

*Laun.* And they have conspired together. I will not
say you shall see a masque, but if you do, then it was not
for nothing that my nose fell a-bleeding on Black Mon-    25
day last at six o'clock i' th' morning, falling out that year
on Ash Wednesday was four year in th' afternoon.

*Shy.* What, are there masques? Hear you me, Jessica.
Lock up my doors; and when you hear the drum
And the vile squealing of the wry-necked fife,    30
Clamber not you up to the casements then,
Nor thrust your head into the public street
To gaze on Christian fools with varnished faces;
But stop my house's ears—I mean my casements.
Let not the sound of shallow fopp'ry enter    35
My sober house. By Jacob's staff I swear
I have no mind of feasting forth tonight;
But I will go. Go you before me, sirrah;
Say I will come.

*Laun.* I will go before, sir. Mistress, look out at win-    40
dow for all this.

          There will come a Christian by
          Will be worth a Jew's eye.          [*Exit.*]

*Shy.* What says that fool of Hagar's offspring? ha?

*Jes.* His words were "Farewell, mistress"—nothing else.    45

*Shy.* The patch is kind enough, but a huge feeder,
Snail-slow in profit, and he sleeps by day

Masquers in seventeenth-century Venice.
From Giacomo Franco,
*Habiti d'huomeni et donne Venetia* (1626).

**II. [vi.]** Near Shylock's house Gratiano and Salerio await Lorenzo, who shortly appears and calls forth Jessica. Antonio then enters with the news that the wind has turned and Bassanio's ship will sail almost immediately.

▬▬▬▬▬▬▬▬▬▬▬▬

1. **penthouse:** a shelter formed by a roof sloping out from a building
6. **Venus' pigeons:** the doves that supposedly drew the chariot of Venus
8. **obliged:** bound by an understanding.
12. **tedious measures:** stately paces that horses were trained to perform

More than the wildcat. Drones hive not with me;
Therefore I part with him, and part with him
To one that I would have him help to waste                    50
His borrowed purse. Well, Jessica, go in.
Perhaps I will return immediately.
Do as I bid you; shut doors after you.
Fast bind, fast find—
A proverb never stale in thrifty mind.          *Exit.*  55
    *Jes.* Farewell; and if my fortune be not crost,
I have a father, you a daughter, lost.

                                                  *Exit.*

[Scene VI. A street in Venice.]

Enter the Masquers, *Gratiano* and *Salerio*.

    *Gra.* This is the penthouse under which Lorenzo
Desired us to make stand.
    *Saler.*                      His hour is almost past.
    *Gra.* And it is marvel he outdwells his hour,
For lovers ever run before the clock.                         5
    *Saler.* O, ten times faster Venus' pigeons fly
To seal love's bonds new-made than they are wont
To keep obliged faith unforfeited!
    *Gra.* That ever holds. Who riseth from a feast
With that keen appetite that he sits down?                    10
Where is the horse that doth untread again
His tedious measures with the unbated fire
That he did pace them first? All things that are
Are with more spirit chased than enjoyed.

15. **younker**: younger, that is, "younger son." The whole passage describes the conduct of a prodigal son, whose means are wasted on loose women.

16. **scarfed**: streaming pennants in the wind like scarves

36. **exchange**: that is, of feminine for masculine dress

How like a younker or a prodigal                    15
The scarfed bark puts from her native bay,
Hugged and embraced by the strumpet wind!
How like the prodigal doth she return,
With over-weathered ribs and ragged sails,
Lean, rent, and beggared by the strumpet wind!     20

                  Enter *Lorenzo.*

  *Saler.* Here comes Lorenzo. More of this hereafter.
  *Lor.* Sweet friends, your patience for my long abode.
Not I, but my affairs, have made you wait.
When you shall please to play the thieves for wives,
I'll watch as long for you then. Approach.          25
Here dwells my father Jew. Ho! who's within?

         [Enter] *Jessica* [in boy's clothes], above.

  *Jes.* Who are you? Tell me for more certainty,
Albeit I'll swear that I do know your tongue.
  *Lor.* Lorenzo, and thy love.
  *Jes.* Lorenzo certain, and my love indeed,       30
For who love I so much? And now who knows
But you, Lorenzo, whether I am yours?
  *Lor.* Heaven and thy thoughts are witness that thou art.
  *Jes.* Here, catch this casket; it is worth the pains.
I am glad 'tis night, you do not look on me,        35
For I am much ashamed of my exchange.
But love is blind, and lovers cannot see
The pretty follies that themselves commit,
For if they could, Cupid himself would blush
To see me thus transformed to a boy.               40
  *Lor.* Descend, for you must be my torchbearer.

43. **light:** "improper," with a pun on **light** meaning "illumination"

44. **'tis an office of discovery:** that is, the function of a torchbearer is to reveal what is going on.

47. **garnish:** adornment

49. **close:** "compact," that is, short in duration, and possibly also "secretive," favorable to concealment

50. **stayed for:** awaited

52. **mo:** more; see I. [i.] 112.

53. **by my hood:** an oath of no precise meaning

54. **Beshrew me:** literally, "curse me," but used as a very mild oath

*Jes.* What, must I hold a candle to my shames?
They in themselves, good sooth, are too too light.
Why, 'tis an office of discovery, love,
And I should be obscured.                                    45
    *Lor.*           So are you, sweet,
Even in the lovely garnish of a boy.
But come at once,
For the close night doth play the runaway,
And we are stayed for at Bassanio's feast.                   50
    *Jes.* I will make fast the doors, and gild myself
With some mo ducats, and be with you straight.
                          *[Exit above.]*
    *Gra.* Now, by my hood, a gentle, and no Jew!
    *Lor.* Beshrew me but I love her heartily;
For she is wise, if I can judge of her;                      55
And fair she is, if that mine eyes be true;
And true she is, as she hath proved herself;
And therefore, like herself, wise, fair, and true,
Shall she be placed in my constant soul.


           [Re-] Enter *Jessica,* [below].


What, art thou come? On, gentlemen! away!                    60
Our masquing mates by this time for us stay.
                  *Exit [with Jessica and Salerio].*


              Enter *Antonio.*


    *Ant.* Who's there?
    *Gra.* Signior Antonio?
    *Ant.* Fie, fie, Gratiano! Where are all the rest?
'Tis nine o'clock; our friends all stay for you.             65
No masque tonight. The wind is come about;

69. **on't:** of it

---

**II. [vii.]** The Prince of Morocco surveys the caskets and chooses the golden one, which contains a death's head with a scroll warning of the folly of being attracted by appearances. He makes a sad departure, to Portia's relief.

---

Stage Dir. **[Flourish cornets]:** this stage direction does not appear here in either the Folio or Quarto texts, but the Folio prints it following the entrance of Salerio and Solanio at the beginning of the next scene. Cornets announce the arrivals of suitors in other scenes.

1. **discover:** reveal

4. **which:** the Folio and Quarto texts read "who" for which. This usage was common enough in Elizabethan practice.

14. **back again:** once more

20. **shows of dross:** objects which appear worthless

Bassanio presently will go aboard.
I have sent twenty out to seek for you.
   *Gra.* I am glad on't, I desire no more delight
Than to be under sail and gone tonight.                    70

                             *Exeunt.*

[Scene VII. Portia's house at Belmont.]


[*Flourish cornets.*] Enter *Portia*, with *Morocco*,
and both their *Trains.*


   *Por.* Go, draw aside the curtains and discover
The several caskets to this noble Prince.
Now make your choice.
   *Mor.* The first, of gold, which this inscription bears,
"Who chooseth me shall gain what many men desire."     5
The second, silver, which this promise carries,
"Who chooseth me shall get as much as he deserves."
This third, dull lead, with warning all as blunt,
"Who chooseth me must give and hazard all he hath."
How shall I know if I do choose the right?                 10
   *Por.* The one of them contains my picture, Prince:
If you choose that, then I am yours withal.
   *Mor.* Some god direct my judgment! Let me see.
I will survey th' inscriptions back again.
What says this leaden casket?                              15
"Who chooseth me must give and hazard all he hath."
Must give—for what? for lead! hazard for lead?
This casket threatens. Men that hazard all
Do it in hope of fair advantages;
A golden mind stoops not to shows of dross;                20

22. **virgin hue:** i.e., the color of the moon, a symbol of virginity

30. **Were:** would be; **disabling:** depreciation

41. **The Hyrcanian deserts:** a wild region south of the Caspian Sea

44. **The watery kingdom:** the ocean

45. **Spets:** spits. The "spit" is the spray thrown heavenward by the breakers.

46. **spirits:** "persons," with a pun on **spirits** (ghosts), which according to popular superstition could not cross bodies of water

49. **like:** likely

51. **cerecloth:** a cloth used for wrapping a corpse; **obscure:** dark, dull

I'll then nor give nor hazard aught for lead.
What says the silver, with her virgin hue?
"Who chooseth me shall get as much as he deserves."
As much as he deserves? Pause there, Morocco,
And weigh thy value with an even hand.                          25
If thou beest rated by thy estimation,
Thou dost deserve enough; and yet enough
May not extend so far as to the lady;
And yet to be afeard of my deserving
Were but a weak disabling of myself.                            30
As much as I deserve? Why, that's the lady!
I do in birth deserve her, and in fortunes,
In graces, and in qualities of breeding;
But more than these, in love I do deserve.
What if I strayed no farther, but chose here?                   35
Let's see once more this saying graved in gold:
"Who chooseth me shall gain what many men desire."
Why, that's the lady! All the world desires her.
From the four corners of the earth they come
To kiss this shrine, this mortal breathing saint.              40
The Hyrcanian deserts and the vasty wilds
Of wide Arabia are as throughfares now
For princes to come view fair Portia.
The watery kingdom, whose ambitious head
Spets in the face of heaven, is no bar                          45
To stop the foreign spirits, but they come,
As o'er a brook, to see fair Portia.
One of these three contains her heavenly picture.
Is't like that lead contains her? 'Twere damnation
To think so base a thought. It were too gross                   50
To rib her cerecloth in the obscure grave.
Or shall I think in silver she's immured,
Being ten times undervalued to tried gold?

An angel.

**56. angel:** the name applied to the coin itself

**66. glisters:** glistens. The phrase was a common proverb, as line 67 indicates.

**70. tombs:** Samuel Johnson's emendation for "timber" in the early texts

**73. inscrolled:** written on a scroll. If he had chosen correctly, he would have found Portia's portrait instead.

**76. heat:** the hot blood of passion. He has vowed to take no other wife and love is henceforth denied him.

**78. part:** depart

O sinful thought! Never so rich a gem
Was set in worse than gold. They have in England          55
A coin that bears the figure of an angel
Stamped in gold, but that's insculped upon;
But here an angel in a golden bed
Lies all within. Deliver me the key:
Here do I choose, and thrive I as I may!                  60
  *Por.* There, take it, Prince, and if my form lie there,
Then I am yours.

                         [*He unlocks the golden casket.*]
  *Mor.*            O hell! what have we here?
A carrion Death, within whose empty eye
There is a written scroll! I'll read the writing.        65

          *All that glisters is not gold—*
          *Often have you heard that told;*
          *Many a man his life hath sold*
          *But my outside to behold;*
          *Gilded tombs do worms infold:*                 70
          *Had you been as wise as bold,*
          *Young in limbs, in judgment old,*
          *Your answer had not been inscrolled.*
          *Fare you well, your suit is cold.*

  Cold indeed, and labor lost.                            75
    Then farewell heat, and welcome frost.
Portia, adieu; I have too grieved a heart
To take a tedious leave; thus losers part.
                         *Exit* [*with his Train*].
  *Por.* A gentle riddance. Draw the curtains, go.
Let all of his complexion choose me so.                   80
                              *Exeunt.*

**II. [viii.]** Salerio and Solanio discuss current gossip: Shylock's reaction to Jessica's elopement (particularly the valuables she carried with her) and a rumor that one of Antonio's ships is lost.

▬▬▬▬▬▬▬

19. **double ducats:** coins worth double the value of ordinary ducats

28. **reasoned:** talked

A Venetian gondola.
From Vecellio, *De gli habiti antichi* (1590).

[Scene VIII. A street in Venice.]

Enter *Salerio* and *Solanio.*

*Saler.* Why, man, I saw Bassanio under sail;
With him is Gratiano gone along;
And in their ship I am sure Lorenzo is not.
*Solan.* The villain Jew with outcries raised the Duke,
Who went with him to search Bassanio's ship.      5
*Saler.* He came too late, the ship was under sail;
But there the Duke was given to understand
That in a gondola were seen together
Lorenzo and his amorous Jessica.
Besides, Antonio certified the Duke                10
They were not with Bassanio in his ship.
*Solan.* I never heard a passion so confused,
So strange, outrageous, and so variable,
As the dog Jew did utter in the streets:
"My daughter! O my ducats! O my daughter!          15
Fled with a Christian! O my Christian ducats!
Justice! the law! My ducats, and my daughter!
A sealed bag, two sealed bags of ducats,
Of double ducats, stol'n from me by my daughter!
And jewels—two stones, two rich and precious stones, 20
Stol'n by my daughter! Justice! Find the girl!
She hath the stones upon her, and the ducats!"
*Saler.* Why, all the boys in Venice follow him,
Crying his stones, his daughter, and his ducats.
*Solan.* Let good Antonio look he keep his day,   25
Or he shall pay for this.
*Saler.*                   Marry, well rememb'red.
I reasoned with a Frenchman yesterday,

A Venetian merchant ship.
From Furtenbach, *Architectura navalis* (1629).

30. **miscarried:** was destroyed
31. **fraught:** freighted, laden
34. **You were best:** you had better, you should
40. **Slubber:** bungle
42. **for:** as for
43. **mind of love:** loving mind
45. **ostents:** shows; see II. [ii.] 187.
49. **affection wondrous sensible:** emotion extremely obvious; that is, an extraordinary display of emotion
53. **embraced heaviness:** the melancholy that he willingly endures (in which he wraps himself)

Who told me, in the narrow seas that part
The French and English there miscarried                    30
A vessel of our country richly fraught.
I thought upon Antonio when he told me,
And wished in silence that it were not his.
   *Solan.* You were best to tell Antonio what you hear.
Yet do not suddenly, for it may grieve him.               35
   *Saler.* A kinder gentleman treads not the earth.
I saw Bassanio and Antonio part.
Bassanio told him he would make some speed
Of his return; he answered, "Do not so.
Slubber not business for my sake, Bassanio,               40
But stay the very riping of the time;
And for the Jew's bond which he hath of me,
Let it not enter in your mind of love.
Be merry, and employ your chiefest thoughts
To courtship, and such fair ostents of love               45
As shall conveniently become you there."
And even there, his eye being big with tears,
Turning his face, he put his hand behind him,
And with affection wondrous sensible
He wrung Bassanio's hand; and so they parted.             50
   *Solan.* I think he only loves the world for him.
I pray thee let us go and find him out,
And quicken his embraced heaviness
With some delight or other.
   *Saler.*                    Do we so.                     55

                       *Exeunt.*

**II.** [**ix.**] Portia is beset by another suitor, the Prince of Arragon. He chooses the silver casket and, finding within the portrait of a "blinking idiot" and a moral, departs. A messenger announces that a gallant envoy for another suitor has arrived and Nerissa expresses the hope that it will prove to be Bassanio.

▪IIIIIIIIIIIIIIIIIIIIIIIIIIIIIIIIII

**4. election:** choice

[Scene IX. Portia's house at Belmont.]

Enter *Nerissa* and a *Servitor.*

*Ner.* Quick, quick, I pray thee; draw the curtain
  straight.
The Prince of Arragon hath ta'en his oath
And comes to his election presently.

*Flourish cornets.* Enter *Arragon,* his *Train,* and *Portia*
        [with her *Train*].

*Por.* Behold, there stand the caskets, noble Prince.    5
If you choose that wherein I am contained,
Straight shall our nuptial rites be solemnized;
But if you fail, without more speech, my lord,
You must be gone from hence immediately.
    *Ar.* I am enjoined by oath to observe three things:    10
First, never to unfold to any one
Which casket 'twas I chose; next, if I fail
Of the right casket, never in my life
To woo a maid in way of marriage;
Lastly,    15
If I do fail in fortune of my choice,
Immediately to leave you and be gone.
    *Por.* To these injunctions every one doth swear
That comes to hazard for my worthless self.
    *Ar.* And so have I addressed me. Fortune now    20
To my heart's hope! Gold, silver, and base lead.
"Who chooseth me must give and hazard all he hath."
You shall look fairer ere I give or hazard.

26-7. **"many" may be meant/ By the fool multi-tude**: that is, "many" may refer to the fool multitude.

28. **fond**: foolish

29. **martlet**: a European martin

31. **in the force and road**: within the power and path

33. **jump with**: coincide with

38. **go about**: undertake

39. **cozen**: cheat

43. **clear**: unblemished

45. **cover that stand bare**: keep on their hats instead of removing them as the lower orders were expected to do before their superiors

48. **seed of honor**: offspring of highborn parents

What says the golden chest? Ha, let me see!
"Who chooseth me shall gain what many men desire."   25
What many men desire! That "many" may be meant
By the fool multitude, that choose by show,
Not learning more than the fond eye doth teach,
Which pries not to th' interior, but, like the martlet,
Builds in the weather on the outward wall,               30
Even in the force and road of casualty.
I will not choose what many men desire,
Because I will not jump with common spirits
And rank me with the barbarous multitude.
Why then, to thee, thou silver treasure house!          35
Tell me once more what title thou dost bear:
"Who chooseth me shall get as much as he deserves."
And well said too, for who shall go about
To cozen Fortune, and be honorable
Without the stamp of merit? Let none presume            40
To wear an undeserved dignity.
O that estates, degrees, and offices
Were not derived corruptly, and that clear honor
Were purchased by the merit of the wearer!
How many then should cover that stand bare!             45
How many be commanded that command!
How much low peasantry would then be gleaned
From the true seed of honor! and how much honor
Picked from the chaff and ruin of the times
To be new varnished! Well, but to my choice.           50
"Who chooseth me shall get as much as he deserves."
I will assume desert. Give me a key for this,
And instantly unlock my fortunes here.
                    [*He unlocks the silver casket.*]
  *Por.* [*Aside*] Too long a pause for that which you find
      there.                                             55

57. **schedule:** scroll

63. **To offend and judge are distinct offices:** that is, "you willingly chose the trial of the caskets; you should not presume to judge the verdict."

66, 67. **tried:** refined

71. **iwis:** certainly; from Middle English *iwis* and Old English *geweiss*

72. **Silvered o'er:** covered with a misleading appearance of value

75. **sped:** finished

81. **wroth:** vexation

83. **deliberate:** logical. They are foolish in thinking that logic will lead them to the correct choice.

84. **wisdom:** Portia characterizes their foolish dependence on logic as **wisdom** because she prefers that they lose.

   *Ar.* What's here? The portrait of a blinking idiot,
Presenting me a schedule! I will read it.
How much unlike art thou to Portia!
How much unlike my hopes and my deservings!
"Who chooseth me shall have as much as he deserves."   60
Did I deserve no more than a fool's head?
Is that my prize? Are my deserts no better?
   *Por.* To offend and judge are distinct offices
And of opposed natures.
   *Ar.*               What is here?   65

> *The fire seven times tried this.*
> *Seven times tried that judgment is*
> *That did never choose amiss.*
> *Some there be that shadows kiss;*
> *Such have but a shadow's bliss.*   70
> *There be fools alive iwis*
> *Silvered o'er, and so was this.*
> *Take what wife you will to bed,*
> *I will ever be your head.*
> *So be gone; you are sped.*   75

> Still more fool I shall appear
> By the time I linger here.
> With one fool's head I came to woo,
> But I go away with two.
> Sweet, adieu. I'll keep my oath,   80
> Patiently to bear my wroth.
>                 *[Exit with his Train.]*

   *Por.* Thus hath the candle singed the moth.
O, these deliberate fools! When they do choose,
They have the wisdom by their wit to lose.

89. **What would my lord:** what do you want with me. Portia is being facetious in dignifying her servant in this way.

93. **sensible regreets:** verbal and material evidence of affection

102. **high-day:** holiday; full of the gaiety provoked by festivity

*Ner.* The ancient saying is no heresy,                    85
Hanging and wiving goes by destiny.
  *Por.* Come draw the curtain, Nerissa.


                    Enter *Messenger.*


  *Mess.* Where is my lady?
  *Por.*                    Here. What would my lord?
  *Mess.* Madam, there is alighted at your gate        90
A young Venetian, one that comes before
To signify th' approaching of his lord;
From whom he bringeth sensible regreets,
To wit, besides commends and courteous breath,
Gifts of rich value. Yet I have not seen               95
So likely an ambassador of love.
A day in April never came so sweet
To show how costly summer was at hand,
As this fore-spurrer comes before his lord.
  *Por.* No more, I pray thee. I am half afeard        100
Thou wilt say anon he is some kin to thee,
Thou spend'st such high-day wit in praising him.
Come, come, Nerissa, for I long to see
Quick Cupid's post that comes so mannerly.
  *Ner.* Bassanio, Lord Love, if thy will it bel      105
                                   *Exeunt.*

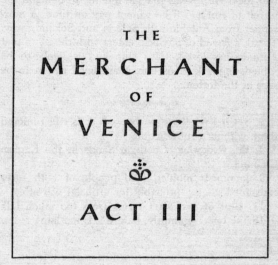

# THE
# MERCHANT
## OF
# VENICE

## ACT III

**III.** [i.] Salerio and Solanio, gossiping again, reveal that another of Antonio's ships has been wrecked. Shylock appears, still bemoaning the loss of his daughter, and relishes the news of Antonio's bad luck. He reveals that he intends to demand the forfeit of Antonio if he cannot pay on time. A messenger from Antonio calls Salerio and Solanio away. Tubal, a friend of Shylock, enters with the news that Antonio has lost a third ship and is likely to be ruined. Shylock plans immediate legal action to be sure of the forfeit.

〰〰〰〰〰〰〰〰〰〰〰

2. **yet it lives there unchecked:** it is still rumored there without contradiction.

4. **the Goodwins:** Goodwin Sands in the English Channel

9. **knapped:** nibbled. Old people of both sexes consumed ginger, probably for artificial warmth.

11. **slips of prolixity:** errors from too much talk

18. **betimes:** promptly, before it is too late

# ACT III

|||||||||||||||||||||||||||||||||||||||||||||||||||||||||||||||||||||||||||||||||||||||||||||||||||||||||||||||||||||

[Scene I. A street in Venice.]

*Enter* Solanio *and* Salerio.

*Solan.* Now what news on the Rialto?

*Saler.* Why, yet it lives there unchecked that Antonio
hath a ship of rich lading wracked on the narrow seas—
the Goodwins I think they call the place—a very dangerous flat, and fatal, where the carcases of many a tall ship    5
lie buried, as they say, if my gossip Report be an honest
woman of her word.

*Solan.* I would she were as lying a gossip in that as
ever knapped ginger or made her neighbors believe she
wept for the death of a third husband. But it is true, with-    10
out any slips of prolixity or crossing the plain highway
of talk, that the good Antonio, the honest Antonio—O that
I had a title good enough to keep his name company!—

*Saler.* Come, the full stop.

*Solan.* Ha, what sayest thou? Why, the end is, he    15
hath lost a ship.

*Saler.* I would it might prove the end of his losses.

*Solan.* Let me say amen betimes, lest the devil cross
my prayer, for here he comes in the likeness of a Jew.

43

A nineteenth-century artist's conception of Shylock.

26. **complexion:** disposition

27. **dam:** parent

29. **if the devil may be her judge:** Salerio implies that only the devil would censure her action and that Shylock is the devil himself.

31-2. **Rebels it at these years:** is it (fleshly passion) still a trial to you at your age. Solanio pretends to misunderstand Shylock's meaning.

36. **Rhenish:** Rhine wine is a white wine

39. **bankrout:** bankrupt

44. **curtsy:** courtesy

48. **hind'red me:** prevented my gaining

Enter *Shylock*.

How now, Shylock? What news among the merchants?  20
    *Shy.* You knew, none so well, none so well as you, of
my daughter's flight.
    *Saler.* That's certain. I, for my part, knew the tailor
that made the wings she flew withal.
    *Solan.* And Shylock, for his own part, knew the bird  25
was fledged; and then it is the complexion of them all to
leave the dam.
    *Shy.* She is damned for it.
    *Saler.* That's certain, if the devil may be her judge.
    *Shy.* My own flesh and blood to rebel!  30
    *Solan.* Out upon it, old carrion! Rebels it at these
years?
    *Shy.* I say my daughter is my flesh and my blood.
    *Saler.* There is more difference between thy flesh and
hers than between jet and ivory; more between your  35
bloods than there is between red wine and Rhenish. But
tell us, do you hear whether Antonio have had any loss
at sea or no?
    *Shy.* There I have another bad match, a bankrout, a
prodigal, who dare scarce show his head on the Rialto, a  40
beggar, that was used to come so smug upon the mart! let
him look to his bond. He was wont to call me usurer: let
him look to his bond. He was wont to lend money for a
Christian curtsy: let him look to his bond.
    *Saler.* Why, I am sure, if he forfeit, thou wilt not take  45
his flesh. What's that good for?
    *Shy.* To bait fish withal. If it will feed nothing else, it
will feed my revenge. He hath disgraced me, and hind'red
me half a million; laughed at my losses, mocked at my

53. **affections:** inclinations

61. **what is his humility:** how much humility does he show. **His** refers to the Christian, of course.

64. **it shall go hard but I will:** it is unlikely that I will not

69-70. **cannot be matched:** cannot match them (Tubal and Shylock)

gains, scorned my nation, thwarted my bargains, cooled     50
my friends, heated mine enemies—and what's his reason?
I am a Jew. Hath not a Jew eyes? Hath not a Jew hands,
organs, dimensions, senses, affections, passions? fed with
the same food, hurt with the same weapons, subject to
the same diseases, healed by the same means, warmed     55
and cooled by the same winter and summer as a Christian
is? If you prick us, do we not bleed? If you tickle us, do
we not laugh? If you poison us, do we not die? And if
you wrong us, shall we not revenge? If we are like you in
the rest, we will resemble you in that. If a Jew wrong a     60
Christian, what is his humility? Revenge. If a Christian
wrong a Jew, what should his sufferance be by Christian
example? Why, revenge. The villainy you teach me I will
execute, and it shall go hard but I will better the instruc-
tion.     65

Enter a *Man* from *Antonio.*

*Man.* Gentlemen, my master Antonio is at his house,
and desires to speak with you both.
*Saler.* We have been up and down to seek him.

Enter *Tubal.*

*Solan.* Here comes another of the tribe. A third cannot
be matched, unless the devil himself turn Jew.     70
                    *Exeunt* [*Solanio, Salerio, and Man*].
*Shy.* How now, Tubal? What news from Genoa? Hast
thou found my daughter?
*Tub.* I often came where I did hear of her, but cannot
find her.

**101-2. cannot choose but break:** cannot avoid going bankrupt

*Shy.* Why, there, there, there, there! A diamond gone   75
cost me two thousand ducats in Frankford! The curse
never fell upon our nation till now; I never felt it till now.
Two thousand ducats in that, and other precious, precious
jewels. I would my daughter were dead at my foot, and
the jewels in her ear: would she were hearsed at my foot,   80
and the ducats in her coffin! No news of them? Why, so—
and I know not what's spent in the search. Why, thou
loss upon loss! the thief gone with so much, and so much
to find the thief, and no satisfaction, no revenge! nor no
ill luck stirring but what lights o' my shoulders; no sighs   85
but o' my breathing; no tears but o' my shedding.

*Tub.* Yes, other men have ill luck too. Antonio, as I
heard in Genoa—

*Shy.* What, what, what? Ill luck, ill luck?

*Tub.* Hath an argosy cast away coming from Tripolis.   90

*Shy.* I thank God, I thank God! Is it true? is it true?

*Tub.* I spoke with some of the sailors that escaped the
wrack.

*Shy.* I thank thee, good Tubal. Good news, good news!
ha, ha! heard in Genoa!   95

*Tub.* Your daughter spent in Genoa, as I heard, one
night fourscore ducats.

*Shy.* Thou stick'st a dagger in me—I shall never see my
gold again—fourscore ducats at a sitting! fourscore ducats!

*Tub.* There came divers of Antonio's creditors in my   100
company to Venice that swear he cannot choose but
break.

*Shy.* I am very glad of it. I'll plague him; I'll torture
him. I am glad of it.

*Tub.* One of them showed me a ring that he had of   105
your daughter for a monkey.

112. **bespeak:** engage

114. **make what merchandise I will:** bargain as I please (on as hard terms as suit me)

━━━━━━━━━━━━━━━━━━━━━━━━━━━━━━━

**III. [ii.]** Portia shows her partiality for Bassanio and urges him to delay selection lest he fail, but he prefers not to continue in uncertainty and to Portia's delight makes the correct choice of the lead casket. Gratiano announces that he and Nerissa wish to be married also. Lorenzo, Jessica, and Salerio interrupt the joyful scene with a letter from Antonio, telling of his ill fortune and hoping that he may see Bassanio before he must pay the forfeit. When Portia learns of the circumstances of the loan, she offers to repay it several times over and urges Bassanio to go to Antonio as soon as their marriage has been performed.

━━━━━━━━━━━━━━━━━━━━━━━━━━━━━━━

6. **quality:** kind

8. **a maiden hath no tongue but thought:** modesty should deny a maiden free expression of her thoughts.

11. **then I am forsworn:** if I did so I would break my sworn oath.

*Shy.* Out upon her! Thou torturest me, Tubal. It was
my turquoise; I had it of Leah when I was a bachelor. I
would not have given it for a wilderness of monkeys.

*Tub.* But Antonio is certainly undone.                    110

*Shy.* Nay, that's true, that's very true. Go, Tubal, fee
me an officer; bespeak him a fortnight before. I will have
the heart of him if he forfeit, for were he out of Venice,
I can make what merchandise I will. Go, Tubal, and meet
me at our synagogue; go, good Tubal; at our synagogue,  115
Tubal.

*Exeunt.*

[Scene II. Portia's house at Belmont.]

Enter *Bassanio, Portia, Gratiano,* [*Nerissa*], and all their
*Trains.*

*Por.* I pray you tarry, pause a day or two
Before you hazard, for in choosing wrong
I lose your company. Therefore forbear awhile.
There's something tells me (but it is not love)
I would not lose you, and you know yourself            5
Hate counsels not in such a quality.
But lest you should not understand me well—
And yet a maiden hath no tongue but thought—
I would detain you here some month or two
Before you venture for me. I could teach you          10
How to choose right, but then I am forsworn.
So will I never be; so may you miss me;
But if you do, you'll make me wish a sin—
That I had been forsworn. Beshrew your eyes!

A noble Venetian lady.
From Vecellio, *De gli habiti antichi* (1590).

15. **o'erlooked**: bewitched

18. **naughty**: wicked; a stronger word then than now

20-1. **Prove it so,/ Let Fortune go to hell for it, not I**: if it prove so (that I cannot actually be yours), the blame must fall on Fortune.

28. **treason**: a jesting reference to the use of the rack to force confession from suspected traitors

30. **fear**: doubt

46. **a swanlike end**: swans were believed to sing when dying.

They have o'erlooked me and divided me; 15
One half of me is yours, the other half yours—
Mine own, I would say, but if mine, then yours,
And so all yours! O, these naughty times
Put bars between the owners and their rights!
And so, though yours, not yours. Prove it so, 20
Let Fortune go to hell for it, not I.
I speak too long, but 'tis to piece the time,
To eke it, and to draw it out in length,
To stay you from election.

    *Bass.*                Let me choose, 25
For as I am, I live upon the rack.

    *Por.* Upon the rack, Bassanio? Then confess
What treason there is mingled with your love.

    *Bass.* None but that ugly treason of mistrust,
Which makes me fear th' enjoying of my love. 30
There may as well be amity and life
'Tween snow and fire as treason and my love.

    *Por.* Ay, but I fear you speak upon the rack,
Where men enforced do speak anything.

    *Bass.* Promise me life, and I'll confess the truth. 35

    *Por.* Well then, confess and live.

    *Bass.*                    "Confess and love"
Had been the very sum of my confession.
O happy torment, when my torturer
Doth teach me answers for deliverance! 40
But let me to my fortune and the caskets.

    *Por.* Away then! I am locked in one of them;
If you do love me, you will find me out.
Nerissa and the rest, stand all aloof.
Let music sound while he doth make his choice; 45
Then, if he lose, he makes a swanlike end,
Fading in music. That the comparison

A Venetian gentleman of high rank.
From Jean de Glen, *Des Habits, Moeurs, etc.* (1601).

48. **my eye shall be the stream**: Portia means that her tears will flow freely.

51. **flourish**: trumpet fanfare

56. **with much more love**: Alcides (Hercules) undertook to rescue Hesione (**the virgin tribute** of line 58) for a reward of horses promised by her father, the King of Troy, not for love of her, as related in Ovid, *Metamorphoses*, Book XI.

59. **stand for sacrifice**: represent the sacrifice (Hesione)

60. **Dardanian**: Trojan

61. **bleared**: tearstained

75. **So may the outward shows be least themselves**: in the same way, external appearance may completely belie an object's true nature.

76. **still**: always; see I. [i.] 17.

May stand more proper, my eye shall be the stream
And wat'ry deathbed for him. He may win;
And what is music then? Then music is                    50
Even as the flourish when true subjects bow
To a new-crowned monarch. Such it is
As are those dulcet sounds in break of day
That creep into the dreaming bridegroom's ear
And summon him to marriage. Now he goes                  55
With no less presence, but with much more love,
Than young Alcides when he did redeem
The virgin tribute paid by howling Troy
To the sea monster. I stand for sacrifice;
The rest aloof are the Dardanian wives,                  60
With bleared visages come forth to view
The issue of th' exploit. Go, Hercules!
Live thou, I live. With much much more dismay
I view the fight than thou that mak'st the fray.

        A Song, the whilst *Bassanio* comments on the
                caskets to himself.

            *Tell me, where is fancy bred,*              65
            *Or in the heart, or in the head?*
            *How begot, how nourished?*
                *Reply, reply.*
            *It is engend'red in the eyes,*
            *With gazing fed, and fancy dies*            70
            *In the cradle where it lies.*
                *Let us all ring fancy's knell.*
                *I'll begin it—Ding, dong, bell.*
*All.*          *Ding, dong, bell.*

  *Bass.* So may the outward shows be least themselves;  75
The world is still deceived with ornament.

81. **approve:** prove

86. **yet:** nevertheless

88. **livers white as milk:** a characteristic of cowards, according to popular belief

89. **excrement:** outgrowth (that is, the beard, as a symbol of virility)

90. **redoubted:** formidable

93. **lightest:** a pun on "light" in the sense of "unchaste"; see II. [vi.] 43.

94. **crisped:** curled

95-6. **Which make such wanton gambols with the wind/ Upon supposed fairness:** with which the wind dallies because of their beautiful appearance

97. **the dowry of a second head:** that is, a wig

99. **guiled:** guileful, treacherous

101. **an Indian beauty:** a woman of dark complexion, who would therefore not meet contemporary English standards of beauty

104. **Hard food for Midas:** a reference to Midas' difficulties when all he touched turned to gold; see Ovid, *Metamorphoses*, Book XI.

105-6. **pale and common drudge/ 'Tween man and man:** that is, the silver casket; silver was used for currency.

106. **meagre:** slight in value

In law, what plea so tainted and corrupt
But, being seasoned with a gracious voice,
Obscures the show of evil? In religion,
What damned error but some sober brow                    80
Will bless it, and approve it with a text,
Hiding the grossness with fair ornament?
There is no vice so simple but assumes
Some mark of virtue on his outward parts.
How many cowards, whose hearts are all as false         85
As stairs of sand, wear yet upon their chins
The beards of Hercules and frowning Mars;
Who, inward searched, have livers white as milk!
And these assume but valor's excrement
To render them redoubted. Look on beauty,                90
And you shall see 'tis purchased by the weight,
Which therein works a miracle in nature,
Making them lightest that wear most of it.
So are those crisped snaky golden locks,
Which make such wanton gambols with the wind             95
Upon supposed fairness, often known
To be the dowry of a second head,
The skull that bred them in the sepulchre.
Thus ornament is but the guiled shore
To a most dangerous sea; the beauteous scarf            100
Veiling an Indian beauty; in a word,
The seeming truth which cunning times put on
To entrap the wisest. Therefore, thou gaudy gold,
Hard food for Midas, I will none of thee;
Nor none of thee, thou pale and common drudge           105
'Tween man and man: but thou, thou meagre lead,
Which rather threaten'st than dost promise aught,
Thy plainness moves me more than eloquence,
And here choose I. Joy be the consequence!

114. **scant:** reduce

119. **Hath come so near creation:** has so nearly produced actual life

122-23. **so sweet a bar/ Should sunder such sweet friends:** such a sweet barrier is the only appropriate one for such sweet friends.

129. **leave itself unfurnished:** leave itself without a second eye in an unfinished portrait, because the painter could no longer see to complete the work

129-32. **how far . . . substance:** just as the gist of my praise does not do justice to the portrait, the portrait fails to do justice to the original. **Substance** in line 132 means the living original.

133. **continent:** used as a synonym for **summary;** that which contains

139. **hold your fortune for your bliss:** regard your fortune as the greatest happiness you can attain

*Por.* [*Aside*] How all the other passions fleet to air,          110
As doubtful thoughts, and rash-embraced despair,
And shudd'ring fear, and green-eyed jealousy!
O love, be moderate; allay thy ecstasy;
In measure rein thy joy; scant this excess!
I feel too much thy blessing: make it less          115
For fear I surfeit!
    *Bass.* [*Opening the leaden casket*] What find I here?
Fair Portia's counterfeit! What demigod
Hath come so near creation? Move these eyes?
Or whether, riding on the balls of mine,          120
Seem they in motion? Here are severed lips,
Parted with sugar breath—so sweet a bar
Should sunder such sweet friends. Here in her hairs
The painter plays the spider, and hath woven
A golden mesh t' entrap the hearts of men          125
Faster than gnats in cobwebs. But her eyes—
How could he see to do them? Having made one,
Methinks it should have power to steal both his
And leave itself unfurnished. Yet look, how far
The substance of my praise doth wrong this shadow          130
In underprizing it, so far this shadow
Doth limp behind the substance. Here's the scroll,
The continent and summary of my fortune.

> *You that choose not by the view*
> *Chance as fair and choose as true.*          135
> *Since this fortune falls to you,*
> *Be content and seek no new.*
> *If you be well pleased with this*
> *And hold your fortune for your bliss,*
> *Turn you where your lady is*          140
> *And claim her with a loving kiss.*

A young Venetian lover.
From Jean de Glen, *Des Habits, Moeurs, etc.* (1601).

143. **by note:** on the authority of the scroll's instructions

144. **prize:** contest

159. **livings:** revenues

160. **account:** calculation

161. **sum of nothing:** Portia explains this with her adjectives "unlessoned," "unschooled," "unpracticed"; **to term in gross:** to itemize

170. **But now:** just an instant ago

172. **even now, but now:** at this very instant

A gentle scroll. Fair lady, by your leave,       [*Kisses her.*]
I come by note, to give and to receive.
Like one of two contending in a prize,
That thinks he hath done well in people's eyes,       145
Hearing applause and universal shout,
Giddy in spirit, still gazing in a doubt
Whether those peals of praise be his or no;
So, thrice-fair lady, stand I, even so,
As doubtful whether what I see be true,       150
Until confirmed, signed, ratified by you.
   *Por.* You see me, Lord Bassanio, where I stand,
Such as I am. Though for myself alone
I would not be ambitious in my wish
To wish myself much better, yet for you       155
I would be trebled twenty times myself,
A thousand times more fair, ten thousand times more rich,
That, only to stand high in your account,
I might in virtues, beauties, livings, friends,
Exceed account. But the full sum of me       160
Is sum of nothing, which, to term in gross,
Is an unlessoned girl, unschooled, unpracticed;
Happy in this, she is not yet so old
But she may learn; happier than this,
She is not bred so dull but she can learn;       165
Happiest of all is that her gentle spirit
Commits itself to yours to be directed,
As from her lord, her governor, her king.
Myself and what is mine to you and yours
Is now converted. But now I was the lord       170
Of this fair mansion, master of my servants,
Queen o'er myself; and even now, but now,
This house, these servants, and this same myself
Are yours, my lord. I give them with this ring,

177. **vantage:** opportunity; **exclaim on you:** rail against you

184. **blent:** blended

185. **wild:** wilderness

202. **intermission:** time wasting

205. **as the matter falls:** as it happens

207. **roof:** that is, roof of the mouth

Which when you part from, lose, or give away,          175
Let it presage the ruin of your love
And be my vantage to exclaim on you.
   *Bass.* Madam, you have bereft me of all words,
Only my blood speaks to you in my veins,
And there is such confusion in my powers          180
As, after some oration fairly spoke
By a beloved prince, there doth appear
Among the buzzing pleased multitude,
Where every something, being blent together,
Turns to a wild of nothing, save of joy,          185
Expressed and not expressed. But when this ring
Parts from this finger, then parts life from hence!
O, then be bold to say Bassanio's dead!
   *Ner.* My lord and lady, it is now our time
That have stood by and seen our wishes prosper          190
To cry "good joy." Good joy, my lord and lady!
   *Gra.* My Lord Bassanio, and my gentle lady,
I wish you all the joy that you can wish;
For I am sure you can wish none from me;
And when your honors mean to solemnize          195
The bargain of your faith, I do beseech you
Even at that time I may be married too.
   *Bass.* With all my heart, so thou canst get a wife.
   *Gra.* I thank your lordship, you have got me one.
My eyes, my lord, can look as swift as yours.          200
You saw the mistress, I beheld the maid;
You loved, I loved; for intermission
No more pertains to me, my lord, than you.
Your fortune stood upon the caskets there,
And so did mine too, as the matter falls;          205
For wooing here until I sweat again,
And swearing till my very roof was dry

211. **Achieved:** won

213. **so you stand:** provided you are

218. **play with them the first boy:** gamble on who has the first boy

226-27. **If that the youth of my new int'rest here/ Have power:** if my newly acquired status here empowers me

228. **very:** true; see II. [ii.] 97.

With oaths of love, at last—if promise last—
I got a promise of this fair one here
To have her love, provided that your fortune      210
Achieved her mistress.
    *Por.*            Is this true, Nerissa?
    *Ner.* Madam, it is, so you stand pleased withal.
    *Bass.* And do you, Gratiano, mean good faith?
    *Gra.* Yes, faith, my lord.      215
    *Bass.* Our feast shall be much honored in your marriage.
    *Gra.* We'll play with them the first boy for a thousand
ducats.
    *Ner.* What, and stake down?      220
    *Gra.* No, we shall ne'er win at that sport, and stake
      down.
But who comes here? Lorenzo and his infidel?
What, and my old Venetian friend Salerio?

Enter *Lorenzo, Jessica,* and *Salerio* [a *Messenger* from
                 Venice].

    *Bass.* Lorenzo and Salerio, welcome hither,      225
If that the youth of my new int'rest here
Have power to bid you welcome. By your leave,
I bid my very friends and countrymen,
Sweet Portia, welcome.
    *Por.*           So do I, my lord.      230
They are entirely welcome.
    *Lor.* I thank your honor. For my part, my lord,
My purpose was not to have seen you here;
But meeting with Salerio by the way,
He did entreat me, past all saying nay,      235
To come with him along.

244. **estate**: state
251. **shrewd**: grievous, extremely distressing

*Saler.*                     I did, my lord,
And I have reason for it. Signior Antonio
Commends him to you.          [*Gives Bassanio a letter.*]
   *Bass.*               Ere I ope his letter,          240
I pray you tell me how my good friend doth.
   *Saler.* Not sick, my lord, unless it be in mind;
Nor well, unless in mind. His letter there
Will show you his estate.      [*Bassanio*] *opens the letter.*
   *Gra.* Nerissa, cheer yond stranger; bid her welcome.  245
Your hand, Salerio. What's the news from Venice?
How doth that royal merchant, good Antonio?
I know he will be glad of our success.
We are the Jasons, we have won the Fleece.
   *Saler.* I would you had won the fleece that he hath lost!  250
   *Por.* There are some shrewd contents in yond same
      paper
That steals the color from Bassanio's cheek:
Some dear friend dead; else nothing in the world
Could turn so much the constitution                   255
Of any constant man. What, worse and worse?
With leave, Bassanio—I am half yourself,
And I must freely have the half of anything
That this same paper brings you.
   *Bass.*                     O sweet Portia,          260
Here are a few of the unpleasant'st words
That ever blotted paper! Gentle lady,
When I did first impart my love to you,
I freely told you all the wealth I had
Ran in my veins—I was a gentleman—                    265
And then I told you true; and yet, dear lady,
Rating myself at nothing, you shall see
How much I was a braggart. When I told you
My state was nothing, I should then have told you

One of "the magnificoes of greatest port."
From Jean de Glen, *Des Habits, Moeurs, etc.* (1601).

271. **engaged:** pledged
272. **mere:** unqualified
284. **present:** ready
287. **confound:** destroy
288. **plies:** solicits
289. **impeach:** cast an imputation on
291. **magnificoes:** Venetian nobility
292. **port:** dignity, weight of influence
293. **envious:** malicious

That I was worse than nothing; for indeed                    270
I have engaged myself to a dear friend,
Engaged my friend to his mere enemy
To feed my means. Here is a letter, lady—
The paper as the body of my friend,
And every word in it a gaping wound                          275
Issuing lifeblood. But is it true, Salerio?
Have all his ventures failed? What, not one hit?
From Tripolis, from Mexico, and England,
From Lisbon, Barbary, and India?
And not one vessel scape the dreadful touch                  280
Of merchant-marring rocks?
  *Saler.*      Not one, my lord.
Besides, it should appear that, if he had
The present money to discharge the Jew,
He would not take it. Never did I know                       285
A creature that did bear the shape of man
So keen and greedy to confound a man.
He plies the Duke at morning and at night,
And doth impeach the freedom of the state
If they deny him justice. Twenty merchants,                  290
The Duke himself, and the magnificoes
Of greatest port have all persuaded with him;
But none can drive him from the envious plea
Of forfeiture, of justice, and his bond.
  *Jes.* When I was with him, I have heard him swear    295
To Tubal and to Chus, his countrymen,
That he would rather have Antonio's flesh
Than twenty times the value of the sum
That he did owe him; and I know, my lord,
If law, authority, and power deny not,                       300
It will go hard with poor Antonio.

325. **dear bought:** that is, acquired under conditions that may cost Antonio his life

*Por.* Is it your dear friend that is thus in trouble?

*Bass.* The dearest friend to me, the kindest man,
The best-conditioned and unwearied spirit
In doing courtesies, and one in whom    305
The ancient Roman honor more appears
Than any that draws breath in Italy.

*Por.* What sum owes he the Jew?

*Bass.* For me three thousand ducats.

*Por.*                         What, no more?    310
Pay him six thousand, and deface the bond.
Double six thousand and then treble that
Before a friend of this description
Shall lose a hair through Bassanio's fault.
First go with me to church and call me wife,    315
And then away to Venice to your friend,
For never shall you lie by Portia's side
With an unquiet soul. You shall have gold
To pay the petty debt twenty times over.
When it is paid, bring your true friend along.    320
My maid Nerissa and myself meantime
Will live as maids and widows. Come, away!
For you shall hence upon your wedding day.
Bid your friends welcome, show a merry cheer;
Since you are dear bought, I will love you dear.    325
But let me hear the letter of your friend.

*Bass. Sweet Bassanio, my ships have all miscarried, my creditors grow cruel, my estate is very low, my bond to the Jew is forfeit, and since in paying it, it is impossible I should live, all debts are cleared between you and I if*  330 *I might but see you at my death. Notwithstanding, use your pleasure: if your love do not persuade you to come, let not my letter.*

**III.** [iii.] Antonio and his jailer interview Shylock in the hope of softening him but he is implacable. Solanio suggests to Antonio that the Duke will disallow the forfeit, but Antonio points out that the reputation of Venice with foreign merchants will be compromised if Shylock can prove injustice. He is resigned to paying the forfeit the next day if only Bassanio will come.

-----

10. **fond**: foolish; see II. [ix.] 28.

*Por.* O love, dispatch all business and be gone!
  *Bass.* Since I have your good leave to go away,     335
I will make haste; but till I come again,
No bed shall e'er be guilty of my stay,
Nor rest be interposer 'twixt us twain.

                                     *Exeunt.*

[Scene III. Before Shylock's house in Venice.]

Enter [*Shylock*] *the Jew* and *Solanio* and *Antonio* and the
                             *Jailer.*

  *Shy.* Jailer, look to him—tell not me of mercy—
This is the fool that lent out money gratis.
Jailer, look to him.
  *Ant.*           Hear me yet, good Shylock.
  *Shy.* I'll have my bond! Speak not against my bond!    5
I have sworn an oath that I will have my bond.
Thou call'dst me dog before thou hadst a cause,
But, since I am a dog, beware my fangs.
The Duke shall grant me justice. I do wonder,
Thou naughty jailer, that thou art so fond          10
To come abroad with him at his request.
  *Ant.* I pray thee hear me speak.
  *Shy.* I'll have my bond. I will not hear thee speak.
I'll have my bond, and therefore speak no more.
I'll not be made a soft and dull-eyed fool,         15
To shake the head, relent, and sigh, and yield
To Christian intercessors. Follow not.
I'll have no speaking; I will have my bond.     *Exit.*

20. **kept:** lived

22. **bootless:** unprofitable, useless

30. **commodity:** favorable business opportunities

31. **it:** referring to "the course of law," line 29. The sense of the passage is that to refuse justice to the holder of the bond (who is an alien) would damage the city's reputation for fair dealing and be discouraging to foreign merchants.

32. **impeach:** discredit; see III. [ii.] 289.

33. **Since that:** since

35. **bated:** abated, diminished

***

**III.** [iv.] Portia leaves her estate in the hands of Lorenzo and Jessica while she and Nerissa supposedly retire to a holy place to pray. She sends a message to her cousin, Dr. Bellario of Padua, and reveals to Nerissa that in male disguise they will see their husbands in Venice.

***

2. **conceit:** conception; see I. [i.] 96.

3. **amity:** friendship

    *Solan.* It is the most impenetrable cur
That ever kept with men.                20
    *Ant.*               Let him alone.
I'll follow him no more with bootless prayers.
He seeks my life. His reason well I know:
I oft delivered from his forfeitures
Many that have at times made moan to me.      25
Therefore he hates me.
    *Solan.*          I am sure the Duke
Will never grant this forfeiture to hold.
    *Ant.* The Duke cannot deny the course of law;
For the commodity that strangers have        30
With us in Venice, if it be denied,
Will much impeach the justice of the state,
Since that the trade and profit of the city
Consisteth of all nations. Therefore go.
These griefs and losses have so bated me      35
That I shall hardly spare a pound of flesh
Tomorrow to my bloody creditor.
Well, jailer, on. Pray God Bassanio come
To see me pay his debt, and then I care not!
                              *Exeunt.*

[Scene IV. Portia's house at Belmont.]


Enter *Portia, Nerissa, Lorenzo, Jessica,* and
    [*Balthasar,*] a Man of *Portia's.*


    *Lor.* Madam, although I speak it in your presence,
You have a noble and a true conceit
Of godlike amity, which appears most strongly

A young Venetian gentleman.
From Vecellio, *De gli habiti antichi* (1590).

9. **Than customary bounty can enforce you:** than any ordinary good deed such as you habitually perform could make you

12. **converse:** associate; **waste:** spend

15. **lineaments:** distinctive characteristics

20. **the semblance of my soul:** the image (Antonio) of my beloved (Bassanio)

33. **deny this imposition:** refuse the responsibility I impose on you

In bearing thus the absence of your lord.
But if you knew to whom you show this honor,                5
How true a gentleman you send relief,
How dear a lover of my lord your husband,
I know you would be prouder of the work
Than customary bounty can enforce you.
    *Por.* I never did repent for doing good,              10
Nor shall not now; for in companions
That do converse and waste the time together,
Whose souls do bear an equal yoke of love,
There must be needs a like proportion
Of lineaments, of manners, and of spirit;                 15
Which makes me think that this Antonio,
Being the bosom lover of my lord,
Must needs be like my lord. If it be so,
How little is the cost I have bestowed
In purchasing the semblance of my soul                    20
From out the state of hellish cruelty!
This comes too near the praising of myself,
Therefore no more of it. Hear other things:
Lorenzo, I commit into your hands
The husbandry and manage of my house                      25
Until my lord's return. For mine own part,
I have toward heaven breathed a secret vow
To live in prayer and contemplation,
Only attended by Nerissa here,
Until her husband and my lord's return.                    30
There is a monastery two miles off,
And there we will abide. I do desire you
Not to deny this imposition,
The which my love and some necessity
Now lays upon you.                                         35

53. **imagined speed:** the speed of thought
54. **Traject:** Florio's *World of Words* (1598) gives the Italian word for ferry as *traghetto*.
63. **accomplished:** furnished
65. **accoutered:** equipped
67. **braver:** finer

   *Lor.*               Madam, with all my heart.
I shall obey you in all fair commands.
   *Por.* My people do already know my mind
And will acknowledge you and Jessica
In place of Lord Bassanio and myself.              40
So fare you well till we shall meet again.
   *Lor.* Fair thoughts and happy hours attend on you!
   *Jes.* I wish your ladyship all heart's content.
   *Por.* I thank you for your wish, and am well pleased
To wish it back on you. Farewell, Jessica.       45
                    *Exeunt [Jessica and Lorenzo].*
Now, Balthasar,
As I have ever found thee honest-true,
So let me find thee still. Take this same letter,
And use thou all th' endeavor of a man
In speed to Padua. See thou render this         50
Into my cousin's hand, Doctor Bellario;
And look, what notes and garments he doth give thee,
Bring them, I pray thee, with imagined speed
Unto the Traject, to the common ferry
Which trades to Venice. Waste no time in words     55
But get thee gone. I shall be there before thee.
   *Balth.* Madam, I go with all convenient speed.   *Exit.*
   *Por.* Come on, Nerissa. I have work in hand
That you yet know not of; we'll see our husbands
Before they think of us.                 60
   *Ner.*             Shall they see us?
   *Por.* They shall, Nerissa, but in such a habit
That they shall think we are accomplished
With that we lack. I'll hold thee any wager,
When we are both accoutered like young men,     65
I'll prove the prettier fellow of the two,
And wear my dagger with the braver grace,

71. **quaint:** skilful, clever; see II. [iv.] 6.
74. **I could not do withal:** I could not help it.
79. **Jacks:** fellows

‖‖‖‖‖‖‖‖‖‖‖‖‖‖‖‖‖‖‖‖‖‖‖‖‖‖‖‖‖‖‖‖‖‖‖‖‖‖

**III.** **[v.]** Launcelot jokes with Jessica and Lorenzo.
Jessica expresses the highest opinion of Portia and
rejoices in Bassanio's luck in winning her.

‖‖‖‖‖‖‖‖‖‖‖‖‖‖‖‖‖‖‖‖‖‖‖‖‖‖

3. **fear you:** fear for you
4. **agitation:** Launcelot probably means "cogita-
tion."

And speak between the change of man and boy
With a reed voice, and turn two mincing steps
Into a manly stride; and speak of frays 70
Like a fine bragging youth; and tell quaint lies,
How honorable ladies sought my love,
Which I denying, they fell sick and died—
I could not do withal! Then I'll repent,
And wish, for all that, that I had not killed them. 75
And twenty of these puny lies I'll tell,
That men shall swear I have discontinued school
Above a twelvemonth. I have within my mind
A thousand raw tricks of these bragging Jacks,
Which I will practice. 80
   *Ner.*                    Why, shall we turn to men?
   *Por.* Fie, what a question's that,
If thou wert near a lewd interpreter!
But come, I'll tell thee all my whole device
When I am in my coach, which stays for us 85
At the park gate; and therefore haste away,
For we must measure twenty miles today.

                                   *Exeunt.*

[Scene V. The garden at Belmont.]

Enter [*Launcelot the*] *Clown* and *Jessica.*

   *Laun.* Yes, truly; for look you, the sins of the father
are to be laid upon the children. Therefore, I promise
you, I fear you. I was always plain with you, and so now
I speak my agitation of the matter. Therefore be o' good
cheer, for truly I think you are damned. There is but one 5

6-7. **but a kind of bastard hope neither:** only a bastard hope at that

14,15. **Scylla, Charybdis:** Scylla, a dangerous rock, and Charybdis, a whirlpool, menace seafarers in the Straits of Messina. The difficulty of escaping both led to a proverbial expression for a hopeless dilemma.

20. **enow:** enough

29. **are out:** have fallen out

hope in it that can do you any good, and that is but a
kind of bastard hope neither.

*Jes.* And what hope is that, I pray thee?

*Laun.* Marry, you may partly hope that your father got
you not—that you are not the Jew's daughter.               10

*Jes.* That were a kind of bastard hope indeed! So the
sins of my mother should be visited upon me.

*Laun.* Truly then I fear you are damned both by
father and mother. Thus when I shun Scylla, your father,
I fall into Charybdis, your mother. Well, you are gone     15
both ways.

*Jes.* I shall be saved by my husband. He hath made
me a Christian.

*Laun.* Truly, the more to blame he! We were Christians
enow before, e'en as many as could well live one by an-    20
other. This making of Christians will raise the price of
hogs. If we grow all to be pork-eaters, we shall not
shortly have a rasher on the coals for money.


### Enter *Lorenzo*.


*Jes.* I'll tell my husband, Launcelot, what you say.
Here he comes.                                             25

*Lor.* I shall grow jealous of you shortly, Launcelot, if
you thus get my wife into corners.

*Jes.* Nay, you need not fear us, Lorenzo, Launcelot
and I are out. He tells me flatly there's no mercy for me
in heaven because I am a Jew's daughter; and he says you  30
are no good member of the commonwealth, for in con-
verting Jews to Christians you raise the price of pork.

*Lor.* I shall answer that better to the commonwealth
than you can the getting up of the Negro's belly: the
Moor is with child by you, Launcelot.                     35

**36-7. more than reason:** larger than is reasonable; **honest:** chaste

**40. the best-grace of wit will shortly turn into silence:** that is, instead of "brevity," "silence" will soon be the soul of wit.

**43. stomachs:** appetites

**46. Only "cover" is the word:** all that remains to be done is to set the table.

**48. Not so, sir, neither:** Launcelot pretends that Lorenzo has suggested that he cover himself, that is, put on his cap, which would not be proper in the presence of his master.

**49. quarrelling with occasion:** quibbling about everything that is said

**56. as humors and conceits shall govern:** according to individual temperaments and whims

**57. suited:** carefully selected for literal application. Note how Launcelot has reversed Lorenzo's directions and promises to serve in the table and cover the meat.

**60. in better place:** that is, higher in society

**61-2. Garnished:** decked out; see II. [vi.] 47; **for a tricksy word/ Defy the matter:** in order to pun, ignore the sense of a conversation

**65. meet:** fitting

*Laun.* It is much that the Moor should be more than
reason; but if she be less than an honest woman, she is
indeed more than I took her for.

*Lor.* How every fool can play upon the word! I think
the best grace of wit will shortly turn into silence, and 40
discourse grow commendable in none only but parrots. Go
in, sirrah; bid them prepare for dinner.

*Laun.* That is done, sir, they have all stomachs.

*Lor.* Goodly Lord, what a wit-snapper are you! Then
bid them prepare dinner. 45

*Laun.* That is done too, sir. Only "cover" is the word.

*Lor.* Will you cover then, sir?

*Laun.* Not so, sir, neither! I know my duty.

*Lor.* Yet more quarrelling with occasion? Wilt thou
show the whole wealth of thy wit in an instant? I pray 50
thee understand a plain man in his plain meaning. Go to
thy fellows, bid them cover the table, serve in the meat,
and we will come in to dinner.

*Laun.* For the table, sir, it shall be served in; for the
meat, sir, it shall be covered; for your coming in to dinner, 55
sir, why, let it be as humors and conceits shall govern.

*Exit.*

*Lor.* O dear discretion, how his words are suited!
The fool hath planted in his memory
An army of good words; and I do know
A many fools, that stand in better place, 60
Garnished like him, that for a tricksy word
Defy the matter. How far'st thou, Jessica?
And now, good sweet, say thy opinion—
How dost thou like the Lord Bassanio's wife?

*Jes.* Past all expressing. It is very meet 65
The Lord Bassanio live an upright life,
For, having such a blessing in his lady,

69. **merit**: the early texts have "mean it" which Alexander Pope corrected to **merit** for the obvious improvement in sense.

84. **set you forth**: praise you at length

He finds the joys of heaven here on earth;
And if on earth he do not merit it,
In reason he should never come to heaven.                    70
Why, if two gods should play some heavenly match,
And on the wager lay two earthly women,
And Portia one, there must be something else
Pawned with the other, for the poor rude world
Hath not her fellow.                                          75

*Lor.*            Even such a husband
Hast thou of me as she is for a wife.

*Jes.* Nay, but ask my opinion too of that!

*Lor.* I will anon. First let us go to dinner.

*Jes.* Nay, let me praise you while I have a stomach.        80

*Lor.* No, pray thee, let it serve for table-talk,
Then, howsome'er thou speak'st, 'mong other things
I shall digest it.

*Jes.*        Well, I'll set you forth.

                                          *Exeunt.*

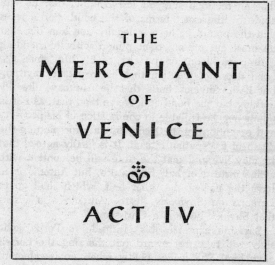

# THE
# MERCHANT
## OF
# VENICE

# ACT IV

**IV.** [i.] Portia and Nerissa, disguised as lawyer and clerk, defend Antonio in court. Shylock's murderous intent becomes clear when he refuses three times the amount of the loan and declines Portia's suggestion that he retain a surgeon lest Antonio die; he will abide by the exact terms of the bond. Portia rules that the pound of flesh is legally due him but that he must cut off an exact pound without shedding a drop of blood, on penalty of his life, since the bond does not mention that he may take anything but flesh. Shylock finds that he can have literally nothing but the bond and, worse than that, as Portia points out, he is liable to confiscation of his property and execution by the Venetian state for plotting the death of a Venetian citizen. It is finally agreed that he may live and that the state will be content with a fine instead of half his wealth, but Antonio is to have the use of the other half, which shall go to Lorenzo on Shylock's death. Antonio also insists that Shylock become a Christian.

Bassanio expresses his gratitude to Portia, who slyly will take no reward but the ring she herself gave him. She leaves coldly when he is reluctant and Bassanio finally sends Gratiano after her with the ring.

▬▬▬▬▬▬▬▬▬▬▬▬▬▬▬

8. **qualify**: dilute, weaken
14. **The very tyranny and rage of his**: his utmost violence and rage

# ACT IV

[Scene I. A courtroom in Venice.]

*Enter the Duke, the Magnificoes, Antonio, Bassanio,*
*Gratiano, [Salerio, and others].*

*Duke.* What, is Antonio here?
*Ant.* Ready, so please your Grace.
*Duke.* I am sorry for thee. Thou art come to answer
A stony adversary, an inhuman wretch,
Uncapable of pity, void and empty                    5
From any dram of mercy.
*Ant.*                       I have heard
Your Grace hath ta'en great pains to qualify
His rigorous course; but since he stands obdurate,
And that no lawful means can carry me                10
Out of his envy's reach, I do oppose
My patience to his fury, and am armed
To suffer with a quietness of spirit
The very tyranny and rage of his.
*Duke.* Go one, and call the Jew into the court.      15
*Saler.* He is ready at the door; he comes, my lord.

The Doge of Venice.
From Vecellio, *De gli habiti antichi* (1590).

19. **leadest this fashion of thy malice:** keep up this pretense of malicious purpose
21. **remorse:** compassion
25. **loose:** release
27. **moiety:** portion
36. **possessed:** informed; see I. [iii.] 61.

### Enter *Shylock*.

*Duke.* Make room, and let him stand before our face.
Shylock, the world thinks, and I think so too,
That thou but leadest this fashion of thy malice
To the last hour of act, and then 'tis thought                    20
Thou'lt show thy mercy and remorse more strange
Than is thy strange apparent cruelty;
And where thou now exacts the penalty,
Which is a pound of this poor merchant's flesh,
Thou wilt not only loose the forfeiture,                          25
But, touched with humane gentleness and love,
Forgive a moiety of the principal,
Glancing an eye of pity on his losses,
That have of late so huddled on his back—
Enow to press a royal merchant down                              30
And pluck commiseration of his state
From brassy bosoms and rough hearts of flint,
From stubborn Turks and Tartars, never trained
To offices of tender courtesy.
We all expect a gentle answer, Jew.                              35
    *Shy.* I have possessed your Grace of what I purpose,
And by our holy Sabbath have I sworn
To have the due and forfeit of my bond.
If you deny it, let the danger light
Upon your charter and your city's freedom!                       40
You'll ask me why I rather choose to have
A weight of carrion flesh than to receive
Three thousand ducats. I'll not answer that!
But say it is my humor, is it answered?
What if my house be troubled with a rat,                         45

"The bagpipe sings i' th' nose."
From the illustration to a broadside ballad.

47. **baned:** poisoned

48. **gaping pig:** a roast pig served with open mouth

51. **affection:** natural inclination; see III. [i.] 53.

52. **sways it:** sways passion

53. **it likes:** affection likes

57. **force:** necessity

61. **certain:** positive, not to be doubted

72. **think you question:** consider that you are debating

74. **bate:** abate; see III. [iii.] 35.

And I be pleased to give ten thousand ducats
To have it baned? What, are you answered yet?
Some men there are love not a gaping pig,
Some that are mad if they behold a cat,
And others, when the bagpipe sings i' th' nose,        50
Cannot contain their urine; for affection,
Master of passion, sways it to the mood
Of what it likes or loathes. Now for your answer:
As there is no firm reason to be rend'red
Why he cannot abide a gaping pig,        55
Why he a harmless necessary cat,
Why he a woollen bagpipe, but of force
Must yield to such inevitable shame
As to offend, himself being offended,
So can I give no reason, nor I will not,        60
More than a lodged hate and a certain loathing
I bear Antonio, that I follow thus
A losing suit against him. Are you answered?
  *Bass.* This is no answer, thou unfeeling man,
To excuse the current of thy cruelty!        65
  *Shy.* I am not bound to please thee with my answer.
  *Bass.* Do all men kill the things they do not love?
  *Shy.* Hates any man the thing he would not kill?
  *Bass.* Every offense is not a hate at first.
  *Shy.* What, wouldst thou have a serpent sting thee   70
    twice?
  *Ant.* I pray you think you question with the Jew.
You may as well go stand upon the beach
And bid the main flood bate his usual height;
You may as well use question with the wolf,        75
Why he hath made the ewe bleat for the lamb;
You may as well forbid the mountain pines

79. **fretten:** fretted, ruffled

84. **with all brief and plain conveniency:** as briefly and simply as is appropriate

106. **Upon:** in accordance with

To wag their high tops and to make no noise
When they are fretten with the gusts of heaven;
You may as well do anything most hard                    80
As seek to soften that—than which what's harder?—
His Jewish heart. Therefore I do beseech you
Make no mo offers, use no farther means,
But with all brief and plain conveniency
Let me have judgment, and the Jew his will.              85
  *Bass.* For thy three thousand ducats here is six.
  *Shy.* If every ducat in six thousand ducats
Were in six parts, and every part a ducat,
I would not draw them, I would have my bond.
   *Duke.* How shalt thou hope for mercy, rend'ring none?   90
  *Shy.* What judgment shall I dread, doing no wrong?
You have among you many a purchased slave,
Which, like your asses and your dogs and mules,
You use in abject and in slavish parts,
Because you bought them. Shall I say to you,             95
"Let them be free, marry them to your heirs!
Why sweat they under burdens? Let their beds
Be made as soft as yours, and let their palates
Be seasoned with such viands"? You will answer,
"The slaves are ours." So do I answer you.              100
The pound of flesh which I demand of him
Is dearly bought, 'tis mine, and I will have it.
If you deny me, fie upon your law!
There is no force in the decrees of Venice.
I stand for judgment. Answer. Shall I have it?          105
  *Duke.* Upon my power I may dismiss this court
Unless Bellario, a learned doctor,
Whom I have sent for to determine this,
Come here today.

117. **wether:** a castrated male sheep

118. **Meetest:** most fit

125. **bankrout:** bankrupt; see III. [i.] 39.

128. **hangman's axe:** the state executioner was known as the hangman, though hanging was only part of some death sentences; **bear:** possess

129. **envy:** malice

131. **inexecrable:** so evil as to be beyond cursing sufficiently

134. **To hold opinion with:** to agree with

*Solan.*          My lord, here stays without          110
A messenger with letters from the doctor,
New come from Padua.
    *Duke.* Bring us the letters. Call the messenger.
    *Bass.* Good cheer, Antonio! What, man, courage yet!
The Jew shall have my flesh, blood, bones, and all,          115
Ere thou shalt lose for me one drop of blood.
    *Ant.* I am a tainted wether of the flock,
Meetest for death. The weakest kind of fruit
Drops earliest to the ground, and so let me.
You cannot better be employed, Bassanio,          120
Than to live still, and write mine epitaph.


    Enter *Nerissa*, [dressed like a *Lawyer's Clerk*].


    *Duke.* Came you from Padua from Bellario?
    *Ner.* From both, my lord. Bellario greets your Grace.
                          [*Presents a letter.*]
    *Bass.* Why dost thou whet thy knife so earnestly?
    *Shy.* To cut the forfeiture from that bankrout there.          125
    *Gra.* Not on thy sole, but on thy soul, harsh Jew,
Thou mak'st thy knife keen; but no metal can—
No, not the hangman's axe—bear half the keenness
Of thy sharp envy. Can no prayers pierce thee?
    *Shy.* No, none that thou hast wit enough to make.          130
    *Gra.* O, be thou damned, inexecrable dog,
And for thy life let justice be accused!
Thou almost mak'st me waver in my faith,
To hold opinion with Pythagoras,
That souls of animals infuse themselves          135
Into the trunks of men. Thy currish spirit
Governed a wolf, who, hanged for human slaughter,

138. **fell:** malevolent

149. **hard by:** near by

164. **let him lack:** cause him to lack

167. **whose trial shall better publish his commendation:** that is, his performance, if he is given the opportunity, will demonstrate his ability better than I can describe it.

Even from the gallows did his fell soul fleet,
And, whilst thou layest in thy unhallowed dam,
Infused itself in thee; for thy desires                              140
Are wolvish, bloody, starved, and ravenous.

  *Shy.* Till thou canst rail the seal from off my bond,
Thou but offend'st thy lungs to speak so loud.
Repair thy wit, good youth, or it will fall
To cureless ruin. I stand here for law.                              145

  *Duke.* This letter from Bellario doth commend
A young and learned doctor to our court.
Where is he?

  *Ner.*        He attendeth here hard by
To know your answer whether you'll admit him.                        150

  *Duke.* With all my heart. Some three or four of you
Go give him courteous conduct to this place.
Meantime the court shall hear Bellario's letter.

  *Your Grace shall understand that at the receipt of your
letter I am very sick; but in the instant that your messen-*          155
*ger came, in loving visitation was with me a young doc-
tor of Rome—his name is Balthasar. I acquainted him
with the cause in controversy between the Jew and Antonio the merchant. We turned o'er many books together.
He is furnished with my opinion, which, bettered with*               160
*his own learning (the greatness whereof I cannot enough
commend), comes with him at my importunity to fill up
your Grace's request in my stead. I beseech you let his
lack of years be no impediment to let him lack a reverend estimation; for I never knew so young a body with*              165
*so old a head. I leave him to your gracious acceptance,
whose trial shall better publish his commendation.*

A doctor of laws.
From Vecellio, *De gli habiti antichi* (1590).

174. **holds this present question:** is the occasion of the present dispute

175. **throughly:** thoroughly

181. **in such rule:** so much within the rules

183. **danger:** power

189. **strained:** constrained

Enter *Portia* for *Balthasar*, [dressed like a
Doctor of Laws].

*Duke.* You hear the learned Bellario what he writes,
And here, I take it, is the doctor come.
Give me your hand. Come you from old Bellario?                    170
  *Por.* I did, my lord.
  *Duke.*                    You are welcome; take your place.
Are you acquainted with the difference
That holds this present question in the court?
  *Por.* I am informed throughly of the cause.                    175
Which is the merchant here? and which the Jew?
  *Duke.* Antonio and old Shylock, both stand forth.
  *Por.* Is your name Shylock?
  *Shy.*                    Shylock is my name.
  *Por.* Of a strange nature is the suit you follow;             180
Yet in such rule that the Venetian law
Cannot impugn you as you do proceed.—
You stand within his danger, do you not?
  *Ant.* Ay, so he says.
  *Por.*                    Do you confess the bond?               185
  *Ant.* I do.
  *Por.*       Then must the Jew be merciful.
  *Shy.* On what compulsion must I? Tell me that.
  *Por.* The quality of mercy is not strained,
It droppeth as the gentle rain from heaven                        190
Upon the place beneath. It is twice blest—
It blesseth him that gives, and him that takes.
'Tis mightiest in the mightiest. It becomes
The throned monarch better than his crown.
His sceptre shows the force of temporal power,                    195
The attribute to awe and majesty,

208. **mitigate the justice of thy plea:** temper with compassion your insistence on severe justice

220. **Wrest once the law to your authority:** this once use your authority to bend the law.

228. **Daniel:** in the Apocryphal Book of Daniel in the King James Version of the Bible, Daniel convicts the elders who had spied on Susanna.

Wherein doth sit the dread and fear of kings;
But mercy is above this sceptred sway,
It is enthroned in the hearts of kings,
It is an attribute to God himself;                            200
And earthly power doth then show likest God's
When mercy seasons justice. Therefore, Jew,
Though justice be thy plea, consider this,
That, in the course of justice, none of us
Should see salvation. We do pray for mercy,                   205
And that same prayer doth teach us all to render
The deeds of mercy. I have spoke thus much
To mitigate the justice of thy plea,
Which if thou follow, this strict court of Venice
Must needs give sentence 'gainst the merchant there.          210
  *Shy.* My deeds upon my head! I crave the law,
The penalty and forfeit of my bond.
  *Por.* Is he not able to discharge the money?
  *Bass.* Yes, here I tender it for him in the court,
Yea, thrice the sum. If that will not suffice,                215
I will be bound to pay it ten times o'er
On forfeit of my hands, my head, my heart.
If this will not suffice, it must appear
That malice bears down truth. And I beseech you,
Wrest once the law to your authority.                         220
To do a great right, do a little wrong,
And curb this cruel devil of his will.
  *Por.* It must not be, there is no power in Venice
Can alter a decree established.
'Twill be recorded for a precedent,                           225
And many an error by the same example
Will rush into the state. It cannot be.
  *Shy.* A Daniel come to judgment! yea, a Daniel!
O wise young judge, how I do honor thee!

A Venetian magistrate.
From Jean de Glen, *Des Habits, Moeurs, etc.* (1601).

248. **stay here on my bond:** await justice according to the terms of my bond

255. **Hath full relation to the penalty:** clearly allows the stipulated penalty

*Por.* I pray you let me look upon the bond.    230
*Shy.* Here 'tis, most reverend Doctor, here it is.
*Por.* Shylock, there's thrice thy money off'red thee.
*Shy.* An oath, an oath, I have an oath in heaven!
Shall I lay perjury upon my soul?
No, not for Venice.    235
*Por.*                Why, this bond is forfeit,
And lawfully by this the Jew may claim
A pound of flesh, to be by him cut off
Nearest the merchant's heart. Be merciful.
Take thrice thy money; bid me tear the bond.    240
*Shy.* When it is paid, according to the tenor.
It doth appear you are a worthy judge;
You know the law, your exposition
Hath been most sound. I charge you by the law,
Whereof you are a well-deserving pillar,    245
Proceed to judgment. By my soul I swear
There is no power in the tongue of man
To alter me. I stay here on my bond.
*Ant.* Most heartily I do beseech the court
To give the judgment.    250
*Por.*                Why then, thus it is:
You must prepare your bosom for his knife.
*Shy.* O noble judge! O excellent young man!
*Por.* For the intent and purpose of the law
Hath full relation to the penalty,    255
Which here appeareth due upon the bond.
*Shy.* 'Tis very true. O wise and upright judge!
How much more elder art thou than thy looks!
*Por.* Therefore lay bare your bosom.
*Shy.*                          Ay, his breast—    260
So says the bond; doth it not, noble judge?
Nearest his heart. Those are the very words.

263. **balance:** scales; a word occasionally used as a plural

266. **on your charge:** at your expense

287-88. **Repent but you . . ./ And he repents not:** you need only regret . . . and he will have no regrets.

290. **with all my heart:** Antonio makes a grim jest; Shylock intends literally to cut his heart out.

*Por.* It is so. Are there balance here to weigh
The flesh?

*Shy.*    I have them ready.                                265

*Por.* Have by some surgeon, Shylock, on your charge,
To stop his wounds, lest he do bleed to death.

*Shy.* Is it so nominated in the bond?

*Por.* It is not so expressed, but what of that?
'Twere good you do so much for charity.                    270

*Shy.* I cannot find it; 'tis not in the bond.

*Por.* You, merchant, have you anything to say?

*Ant.* But little. I am armed and well prepared.
Give me your hand, Bassanio. Fare you well!
Grieve not that I am fall'n to this for you;              275
For herein Fortune shows herself more kind
Than is her custom. It is still her use
To let the wretched man outlive his wealth
To view with hollow eye and wrinkled brow
An age of poverty; from which ling'ring penance           280
Of such misery doth she cut me off.
Commend me to your honorable wife;
Tell her the process of Antonio's end;
Say how I loved you, speak me fair in death;
And when the tale is told, bid her be judge               285
Whether Bassanio had not once a love.
Repent but you that you shall lose your friend,
And he repents not that he pays your debt;
For if the Jew do cut but deep enough,
I'll pay it instantly with all my heart.                  290

*Bass.* Antonio, I am married to a wife
Which is as dear to me as life itself,
But life itself, my wife, and all the world
Are not with me esteemed above thy life.
I would lose all, ay, sacrifice them all                  295

A "grand capitaine de Justice" of the Venetian state.
From Jean de Glen, *Des Habits, Moeurs, etc.* (1601).

306. **Barabbas:** a thief condemned before Pontius
Pilate; see Mark 15:6-11.

Here to this devil, to deliver you.

   *Por.* Your wife would give you little thanks for that
If she were by to hear you make the offer.

   *Gra.* I have a wife who I protest I love.
I would she were in heaven, so she could          300
Entreat some power to change this currish Jew.

   *Ner.* 'Tis well you offer it behind her back.
The wish would make else an unquiet house.

   *Shy.* [*Aside*] These be the Christian husbands! I have
     a daughter—          305
Would any of the stock of Barabbas
Had been her husband rather than a Christian!—
We trifle time. I pray thee pursue sentence.

   *Por.* A pound of that same merchant's flesh is thine.
The court awards it, and the law doth give it.       310

   *Shy.* Most rightful judge!

   *Por.* And you must cut this flesh from off his breast.
The law allows it, and the court awards it.

   *Shy.* Most learned judge! A sentence! Come, prepare!

   *Por.* Tarry a little; there is something else.      315
This bond doth give thee here no jot of blood;
The words expressly are "a pound of flesh."
Take then thy bond, take thou thy pound of flesh;
But in the cutting it if thou dost shed
One drop of Christian blood, thy lands and goods    320
Are, by the laws of Venice, confiscate
Unto the state of Venice.

   *Gra.* O upright judge! Mark, Jew. O learned judge!

   *Shy.* Is that the law?

   *Por.*              Thyself shalt see the act;    325
For, as thou urgest justice, be assured
Thou shalt have justice more than thou desir'st.

333. **all:** nothing but

342. **scruple:** an ancient Roman unit of weight equivalent to one twenty-fourth of an ounce

346. **on the hip:** at my mercy; see I. [iii.] 42.

358. **stay no longer question:** remain for no further argument

    *Gra.* O learned judge! Mark, Jew. A learned judge!

    *Shy.* I take this offer then. Pay the bond thrice,

And let the Christian go. 330

    *Bass.*               Here is the money.

    *Por.* Soft!

The Jew shall have all justice. Soft! no haste.

He shall have nothing but the penalty.

    *Gra.* O Jew! an upright judge! a learned judge! 335

    *Por.* Therefore prepare thee to cut off the flesh.

Shed thou no blood, nor cut thou less nor more

But just a pound of flesh. If thou tak'st more

Or less than a just pound—be it but so much

As makes it light or heavy in the substance 340

Or the division of the twentieth part

Of one poor scruple; nay, if the scale do turn

But in the estimation of a hair—

Thou diest, and all thy goods are confiscate.

    *Gra.* A second Daniel! a Daniel, Jew! 345

Now, infidel, I have you on the hip.

    *Por.* Why doth the Jew pause? Take thy forfeiture.

    *Shy.* Give me my principal, and let me go.

    *Bass.* I have it ready for thee; here it is.

    *Por.* He hath refused it in the open court. 350

He shall have merely justice and his bond.

    *Gra.* A Daniel still say I, a second Daniel!

I thank thee, Jew, for teaching me that word.

    *Shy.* Shall I not have barely my principal?

    *Por.* Thou shalt have nothing but the forfeiture, 355

To be so taken at thy peril, Jew.

    *Shy.* Why, then the devil give him good of it!

I'll stay no longer question.

    *Por.*              Tarry, Jew,

The law hath yet another hold on you. 360

362. **an alien:** it must be remembered that, as a non-Christian, Shylock could not become a citizen of Venice.

370. **predicament:** situation; formerly the word did not imply calamity, as in modern usage.

375. **rehearsed:** enumerated

385. **humbleness may drive unto a fine:** humble behavior on your part may reduce to a mere fine

It is enacted in the laws of Venice,
If it be proved against an alien
That by direct or indirect attempts
He seek the life of any citizen,
The party 'gainst the which he doth contrive               365
Shall seize one half his goods; the other half
Comes to the privy coffer of the state;
And the offender's life lies in the mercy
Of the Duke only, 'gainst all other voice.
In which predicament I say thou stand'st;                  370
For it appears by manifest proceeding
That indirectly, and directly too,
Thou hast contrived against the very life
Of the defendant, and thou hast incurred
The danger formerly by me rehearsed.                       375
Down, therefore, and beg mercy of the Duke.
  *Gra.* Beg that thou mayst have leave to hang thyself!
And yet, thy wealth being forfeit to the state,
Thou hast not left the value of a cord;
Therefore thou must be hanged at the state's charge.       380
  *Duke.* That thou shalt see the difference of our spirit,
I pardon thee thy life before thou ask it.
For half thy wealth, it is Antonio's;
The other half comes to the general state,
Which humbleness may drive unto a fine.                    385
  *Por.* Ay, for the state, not for Antonio.
  *Shy.* Nay, take my life and all! Pardon not that!
You take my house when you do take the prop
That doth sustain my house; you take my life
When you do take the means whereby I live.                 390
  *Por.* What mercy can you render him, Antonio?
  *Gra.* A halter gratis. Nothing else, for God's sake!

393-98. Antonio is saying that if the Duke and the court will be satisfied with a fine instead of taking half of Shylock's goods, he himself will be satisfied with the use of the half due him, which should revert to Jessica's husband on the death of Shylock.

400. **presently:** at once

414. **ten more:** that is, a total of "twelve just men" as a jury to condemn him to death

421. **gratify this gentleman:** that is, give Balthasar a reward.

*Ant.* So please my lord the Duke and all the court
To quit the fine for one half of his goods,
I am content; so he will let me have                    395
The other half in use, to render it
Upon his death unto the gentleman
That lately stole his daughter—
Two things provided more: that, for this favor,
He presently become a Christian;                        400
The other, that he do record a gift
Here in the court of all he dies possessed
Unto his son Lorenzo and his daughter.
    *Duke.* He shall do this, or else I do recant
The pardon that I late pronounced here.                 405
    *Por.* Art thou contented, Jew? What dost thou say?
    *Shy.* I am content.
    *Por.*                    Clerk, draw a deed of gift.
    *Shy.* I pray you give me leave to go from hence.
I am not well. Send the deed after me,                  410
And I will sign it.
    *Duke.*          Get thee gone, but do it.
    *Gra.* In christ'ning shalt thou have two godfathers.
Had I been judge, thou shouldst have had ten more,
To bring thee to the gallows, not the font.             415
                                    *Exit* [*Shylock*].
    *Duke.* Sir, I entreat you home with me to dinner.
    *Por.* I humbly do desire your Grace of pardon.
I must away this night toward Padua,
And it is meet I presently set forth.
    *Duke.* I am sorry that your leisure serves you not.  420
Antonio, gratify this gentleman,
For in my mind you are much bound to him.
                        *Exeunt Duke and his Train.*

427. **cope:** repay

434. **know me when we meet again:** on the surface Portia means only that she as Balthasar would like to continue friendship with Bassanio, but she has her tongue in her cheek because he will not know her as Balthasar when next they meet.

442. **for your love:** as Balthasar, Portia means only "as a token of friendship," but the phrase is more meaningful because she gave it to Bassanio as a love token.

*Bass.* Most worthy gentleman, I and my friend
Have by your wisdom been this day acquitted
Of grievous penalties, in lieu whereof,                                   425
Three thousand ducats, due unto the Jew,
We freely cope your courteous pains withal.

*Ant.* And stand indebted, over and above,
In love and service to you evermore.

*Por.* He is well paid that is well satisfied;                            430
And I, delivering you, am satisfied,
And therein do account myself well paid.
My mind was never yet more mercenary.
I pray you know me when we meet again.
I wish you well, and so I take my leave.                                   435

*Bass.* Dear sir, of force I must attempt you further.
Take some remembrance of us as a tribute,
Not as a fee. Grant me two things, I pray you—
Not to deny me, and to pardon me.

*Por.* You press me far, and therefore I will yield.                       440
Give me your gloves, I'll wear them for your sake;
And for your love I'll take this ring from you.
Do not draw back your hand, I'll take no more,
And you in love shall not deny me this.

*Bass.* This ring, good sir? Alas, it is a trifle!                         445
I will not shame myself to give you this.

*Por.* I will have nothing else but only this;
And now methinks I have a mind to it.

*Bass.* There's more depends on this than on the value.
The dearest ring in Venice will I give you,                                450
And find it out by proclamation.
Only for this, I pray you pardon me.

*Por.* I see, sir, you are liberal in offers.
You taught me first to beg, and now methinks
You teach me how a beggar should be answered.                              455

**IV. [ii.]** Gratiano overtakes Portia and Nerissa and delivers the ring. Nerissa determines to see if she cannot wheedle her own ring from him.

▬▬▬▬▬▬▬▬▬▬▬▬▬▬▬▬▬▬▬▬

*Bass.* Good sir, this ring was given me by my wife,
And when she put it on, she made me vow
That I should neither sell nor give nor lose it.
   *Por.* That 'scuse serves many men to save their gifts,
And if your wife be not a madwoman,                    460
And know how well I have deserved this ring,
She would not hold out enemy forever
For giving it to me. Well, peace be with you!
                    *Exeunt [Portia and Nerissa].*
   *Ant.* My Lord Bassanio, let him have the ring.
Let his deservings, and my love withal,                 465
Be valued 'gainst your wive's commandment.
   *Bass.* Go, Gratiano, run and overtake him.
Give him the ring and bring him, if thou canst,
Unto Antonio's house. Away! make haste.
                    *Exit Gratiano.*
Come, you and I will thither presently,                 470
And in the morning early will we both
Fly toward Belmont. Come, Antonio.

                          *Exeunt.*

---

[Scene II. A street in Venice.]


Enter *Portia* and *Nerissa.*


   *Por.* Inquire the Jew's house out, give him this deed,
And let him sign it. We'll away tonight
And be a day before our husbands home.
This deed will be well welcome to Lorenzo.

5. **you are well o'erta'en**: overtaking you is a happy chance.

6. **upon more advice**: after further consideration

18. **old**: abundant; see I. [i.] 84.

Enter *Gratiano*.

*Gra.* Fair sir, you are well o'erta'en.                          5
My Lord Bassanio, upon more advice,
Hath sent you here this ring, and doth entreat
Your company at dinner.
*Por.*                    That cannot be.
His ring I do accept most thankfully,                            10
And so I pray you tell him. Furthermore,
I pray you show my youth old Shylock's house.
*Gra.* That will I do.
*Ner.*                  Sir, I would speak with you.
[*Aside to Portia*] I'll see if I can get my husband's ring,     15
Which I did make him swear to keep forever.
*Por.* [*Aside to Nerissa*] Thou mayst, I warrant. We
    shall have old swearing
That they did give the rings away to men;
But we'll outface them, and outswear them too.                   20
[*Aloud*] Away! make haste. Thou know'st where I will
    tarry.
*Ner.* Come, good sir, will you show me to this house?
                                          *Exeunt.*

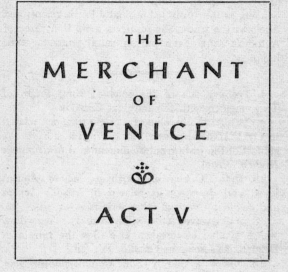

THE
MERCHANT
OF
VENICE

ACT V

**V.** [i.] Lorenzo and Jessica are enjoying the night air at Belmont when Portia, Nerissa, Bassanio, and Gratiano arrive, almost simultaneously. After preliminary greetings, the two women pretend to be angry because their rings have been given away (to women, as they insist), but finally Portia relents and discloses the truth. She also has news that three of Antonio's ships have put in safely, and all ends happily.

▬▬▬▬▬▬▬▬▬▬▬▬

4. **Troilus:** one of the sons of King Priam of Troy, in love with the faithless Cressida

8. **Thisbe:** the heroine of a tragic romance related in Ovid, *Metamorphoses*, Book IV. Her story is the subject of the rustics' entertainment in *A Midsummer Night's Dream*.

12. **Dido:** Queen of Carthage, whom Aeneas loved and deserted, as related in Virgil's *Aeneid* and retold by various other writers

13. **waft:** waved (the willow wand). The willow was a symbol of forsaken love. See the refrain of Desdemona's song in *Othello*, IV, [iii.]

16. **Medea:** as told by Ovid, *Metamorphoses*, Book VII.

# ACT V

▬▬▬▬▬▬▬▬▬▬▬▬▬▬▬▬▬▬▬▬▬▬▬▬▬▬▬▬▬▬▬▬▬▬▬▬▬▬▬▬▬▬▬▬▬▬▬▬▬▬

[Scene I. The grounds before Portia's house at Belmont.]

Enter *Lorenzo* and *Jessica*.

*Lor.* The moon shines bright. In such a night as this,
When the sweet wind did gently kiss the trees
And they did make no noise—in such a night
Troilus methinks mounted the Trojan walls
And sighed his soul toward the Grecian tents,    5
Where Cressid lay that night.
*Jes.*                           In such a night
Did Thisbe fearfully o'ertrip the dew,
And saw the lion's shadow ere himself,
And ran dismayed away.                           10
*Lor.*                    In such a night
Stood Dido with a willow in her hand
Upon the wild sea-banks, and waft her love
To come again to Carthage.
*Jes.*                           In such a night    15
Medea gathered the enchanted herbs
That did renew old Æson.

19. **steal:** she left secretly and literally stole money and jewels from her father.

20. **with an unthrift love:** that is, motivated by a love which did not value material fortune

 *Lor.*     In such a night
Did Jessica steal from the wealthy Jew,
And with an unthrift love did run from Venice   20
As far as Belmont.
 *Jes.*   In such a night
Did young Lorenzo swear he loved her well,
Stealing her soul with many vows of faith,
And ne'er a true one.         25
 *Lor.*     In such a night
Did pretty Jessica (like a little shrew)
Slander her love, and he forgave it her.
 *Jes.* I would out-night you, did no body come;
But, hark, I hear the footing of a man.   30

*Enter a Messenger.*

 *Lor.* Who comes so fast in silence of the night?
 *Mess.* A friend.
 *Lor.* A friend? What friend? Your name, I pray you,
  friend?
 *Mess.* Stephano is my name, and I bring word   35
My mistress will before the break of day
Be here at Belmont. She doth stray about
By holy crosses, where she kneels and prays
For happy wedlock hours.
 *Lor.*    Who comes with her?   40
 *Mess.* None but a holy hermit and her maid.
I pray you, is my master yet returned?
 *Lor.* He is not, nor we have not heard from him.
But go we in, I pray thee, Jessica,
And ceremoniously let us prepare     45
Some welcome for the mistress of the house.

54. **post:** messenger

65. **touches of sweet harmony:** a stringed instrument was said to be touched when played.

67. **patens:** tiles

70. **quiring:** choiring, acting as a choir; **young-eyed cherubins:** bright-eyed angels

72. **muddy vesture of decay:** the clothing of mortal flesh

Enter [*Launcelot, the*] *Clown.*

*Laun.* Sola, sola! wo ha, ho! sola, sola!

*Lor.* Who calls?

*Laun.* Sola! Did you see Master Lorenzo and Mistress
Lorenzo? Sola, sola!                                             50

*Lor.* Leave holloaing, man! Here.

*Laun.* Sola! Where? where?

*Lor.* Here!

*Laun.* Tell him there's a post come from my master,
with his horn full of good news. My master will be here   55
ere morning.                                        [*Exit.*]

*Lor.* Sweet soul, let's in, and there expect their coming.
And yet no matter. Why should we go in?
My friend Stephano, signify, I pray you,
Within the house, your mistress is at hand                  60
And bring your music forth into the air.

                                        [*Exit Stephano.*]

How sweet the moonlight sleeps upon this bank!
Here will we sit and let the sounds of music
Creep in our ears. Soft stillness and the night
Become the touches of sweet harmony.                        65
Sit, Jessica. Look how the floor of heaven
Is thick inlaid with patens of bright gold.
There's not the smallest orb which thou behold'st
But in his motion like an angel sings,
Still quiring to the young-eyed cherubins;                  70
Such harmony is in immortal souls;
But whilst this muddy vesture of decay
Doth grossly close it in, we cannot hear it.

Diana as the moon goddess.
From Vincenzo Cartari,
*Imagini delli Dei de gl'Antichi* (1674).

74. **Diana**: the moon goddess of classical mythology

81. **fetching**: performing

87. **the poet**: more than one classical poet told of the power of Orpheus' music, but most likely Ovid is meant, since many allusions indicate that Shakespeare was familiar with his *Metamorphoses*.

88. **drew**: that is, attracted them by his music

89. **stockish**: like a stock, stolid

93. **stratagems**: violent deeds; **spoils**: acts of plunder

95. **Erebus**: a dark underground region on the route to Hades, in Greek mythology

[Enter *Musicians*.]

Come, ho, and wake Diana with a hymn!
With sweetest touches pierce your mistress' ear          75
And draw her home with music.

                                        *Play music.*

  *Jes.* I am never merry when I hear sweet music.
  *Lor.* The reason is, your spirits are attentive.
For do but note a wild and wanton herd,
Or race of youthful and unhandled colts,                 80
Fetching mad bounds, bellowing and neighing loud,
Which is the hot condition of their blood:
If they but hear perchance a trumpet sound,
Or any air of music touch their ears,
You shall perceive them make a mutual stand,            85
Their savage eyes turned to a modest gaze
By the sweet power of music. Therefore the poet
Did feign that Orpheus drew trees, stones, and floods,
Since naught so stockish, hard, and full of rage
But music for the time doth change his nature.          90
The man that hath no music in himself,
Nor is not moved with concord of sweet sounds,
Is fit for treasons, stratagems, and spoils;
The motions of his spirit are dull as night,
And his affections dark as Erebus.                       95
Let no such man be trusted. Mark the music.

Enter *Portia* and *Nerissa*.

  *Por.* That light we see is burning in my hall.
How far that little candle throws his beams!
So shines a good deed in a naughty world.

105. **main of waters:** ocean

107. **respect:** that is, respect of circumstances. Portia probably means the circumstances of the beautiful night as well as her happy return to husband and home after her successful venture.

111. **attended:** accompanied (by a competing singer)

115. **by season seasoned are:** by happening seasonably (at the right moment) are increased in savor

117. **Endymion:** the beloved of Selene, another name for the moon goddess in Greek mythology

125. **speed:** prosper

*Ner.* When the moon shone, we did not see the candle.  100
 *Por.* So doth the greater glory dim the less.
A substitute shines brightly as a king
Until a king be by, and then his state
Empties itself, as doth an inland brook
Into the main of waters. Music! hark!  105
 *Ner.* It is your music, madam, of the house.
 *Por.* Nothing is good, I see, without respect.
Methinks it sounds much sweeter than by day.
 *Ner.* Silence bestows that virtue on it, madam.
 *Por.* The crow doth sing as sweetly as the lark  110
When neither is attended; and I think
The nightingale, if she should sing by day
When every goose is cackling, would be thought
No better a musician than the wren.
How many things by season seasoned are  115
To their right praise and true perfection!
Peace—how the moon sleeps with Endymion,
And would not be awaked.

         *Music ceases.*
 *Lor.*      That is the voice,
Or I am much deceived, of Portia.  120
 *Por.* He knows me as the blind man knows the cuckoo,
By the bad voice.
 *Lor.*   Dear lady, welcome home.
 *Por.* We have been praying for our husbands' welfare,
Which speed, we hope, the better for our words.  125
Are they returned?
 *Lor.*   Madam, they are not yet;
But there is come a messenger before
To signify their coming.
 *Por.*    Go in, Nerissa.  130

139. **We should hold day with the Antipodes:** daylight would prevail here when the sun was lighting the Antipodes, the other side of the world.

142. **light:** unchaste; see the similar use at II. [vi.] 43; **heavy:** sorrowful

144. **God sort all:** may God determine it as He sees fit.

148. **You should in all sense:** you have every reason to

153. **scant this breathing courtesy:** cut short polite verbiage

157. **gelt:** gelded, castrated

Give order to my servants that they take
No note at all of our being absent hence—
Nor you, Lorenzo—Jessica, nor you.

*A tucket sounds.*

*Lor.* Your husband is at hand; I hear his trumpet.
We are no telltales, madam; fear you not.                    135
*Por.* This night methinks is but the daylight sick;
It looks a little paler. 'Tis a day
Such as the day is when the sun is hid.

Enter *Bassanio, Antonio, Gratiano,* and their *Followers.*

*Bass.* We should hold day with the Antipodes
If you would walk in absence of the sun.                     140
*Por.* Let me give light, but let me not be light,
For a light wife doth make a heavy husband,
And never be Bassanio so for me.
But God sort all! You are welcome home, my lord.
*Bass.* I thank you, madam. Give welcome to my friend.  145
This is the man, this is Antonio,
To whom I am so infinitely bound.
*Por.* You should in all sense be much bound to him,
For, as I hear, he was much bound for you.
*Ant.* No more than I am well acquitted of.                 150
*Por.* Sir, you are very welcome to our house.
It must appear in other ways than words,
Therefore I scant this breathing courtesy.
*Gra.* [*To Nerissa*] By yonder moon I swear you do me
      wrong!                                                 155
In faith, I gave it to the judge's clerk.
Would he were gelt that had it, for my part,
Since you do take it, love, so much at heart.
*Por.* A quarrel, ho, already! What's the matter?

161. **posy:** rhymed inscription
169. **respective:** mindful
175. **scrubbed:** stunted
177. **prating:** boastful
189. **mad:** frantic
190. **I were best:** it would be best for me

*Gra.* About a hoop of gold, a paltry ring          160
That she did give to me, whose posy was
For all the world like cutler's poetry
Upon a knife, "Love me, and leave me not."
    *Ner.* What talk you of the posy or the value?
You swore to me, when I did give it you,          165
That you would wear it till your hour of death,
And that it should lie with you in your grave.
Though not for me, yet for your vehement oaths,
You should have been respective and have kept it.
Gave it a judge's clerk! No, God's my judge,          170
The clerk will ne'er wear hair on's face that had it.
    *Gra.* He will, an if he live to be a man.
    *Ner.* Ay, if a woman live to be a man.
    *Gra.* Now, by this hand, I gave it to a youth,
A kind of boy, a little scrubbed boy,          175
No higher than thyself, the judge's clerk,
A prating boy that begged it as a fee.
I could not for my heart deny it him.
    *Por.* You were to blame—I must be plain with you—
To part so slightly with your wife's first gift,          180
A thing stuck on with oaths upon your finger
And so riveted with faith unto your flesh.
I gave my love a ring, and made him swear
Never to part with it, and here he stands:
I dare be sworn for him he would not leave it          185
Nor pluck it from his finger for the wealth
That the world masters. Now, in faith, Gratiano,
You give your wife too unkind a cause of grief.
An 'twere to me, I should be mad at it.
    *Bass.* [*Aside*] Why, I were best to cut my left hand off          190
And swear I lost the ring defending it.

211. **conceive:** understand correctly

217. **contain:** retain

221. **wanted:** lacked

222. **urge:** insist upon; **ceremony:** formality (formal symbol of faith)

224. **I'll die for't but some woman had the ring:** I'll stake my life that some woman received the ring.

*Gra.* My Lord Bassanio gave his ring away
Unto the judge that begged it, and indeed
Deserved it too; and then the boy, his clerk,
That took some pains in writing, he begged mine;     195
And neither man nor master would take aught
But the two rings.
    *Por.*          What ring gave you, my lord?
Not that, I hope, which you received of me.
    *Bass.* If I could add a lie unto a fault,     200
I would deny it; but you see my finger
Hath not the ring upon it—it is gone.
    *Por.* Even so void is your false heart of truth.
By heaven, I will ne'er come in your bed
Until I see the ring!     205
    *Ner.*          Nor I in yours
Till I again see mine!
    *Bass.*          Sweet Portia,
If you did know to whom I gave the ring,
If you did know for whom I gave the ring,     210
And would conceive for what I gave the ring,
And how unwillingly I left the ring
When naught would be accepted but the ring,
You would abate the strength of your displeasure.
    *Por.* If you had known the virtue of the ring,     215
Or half her worthiness that gave the ring,
Or your own honor to contain the ring,
You would not then have parted with the ring.
What man is there so much unreasonable,
If you had pleased to have defended it     220
With any terms of zeal, wanted the modesty
To urge the thing held as a ceremony?
Nerissa teaches me what to believe.
I'll die for't but some woman had the ring!

226. **civil doctor:** doctor of law

230. **held up:** defended

242. **liberal:** "free" in the sense of generous and "licentious"

246. **Argus:** a giant with a hundred eyes, whom Juno set to guard Io from Zeus, in Greek mythology

250. **be well advised:** be warned

*Bass.* No, by my honor, madam, by my soul,                    225
No woman had it, but a civil doctor,
Which did refuse three thousand ducats of me
And begged the ring; the which I did deny him,
And suffered him to go displeased away,
Even he that had held up the very life                         230
Of my dear friend. What should I say, sweet lady?
I was enforced to send it after him.
I was beset with shame and courtesy.
My honor would not let ingratitude
So much besmear it. Pardon me, good lady,                      235
For, by these blessed candles of the night,
Had you been there, I think you would have begged
The ring of me to give the worthy doctor.
    *Por.* Let not that doctor e'er come near my house.
Since he hath got the jewel that I loved,                      240
And that which you did swear to keep for me,
I will become as liberal as you;
I'll not deny him anything I have,
No, not my body, nor my husband's bed.
Know him I shall, I am well sure of it.                        245
Lie not a night from home; watch me like Argus.
If you do not, if I be left alone,
Now, by mine honor, which is yet mine own,
I'll have that doctor for my bedfellow.
    *Ner.* And I his clerk. Therefore be well advised           250
How you do leave me to mine own protection.
    *Gra.* Well, do you so. Let not me take him then,
For if I do, I'll mar the young clerk's pen.
    *Ant.* I am th' unhappy subject of these quarrels.
    *Por.* Sir, grieve not you. You are welcome notwith- 255
    standing.

257. **enforced wrong**: wrong which I could not help

264. **oath of credit**: credible oath

268. **for his wealth**: to enrich him

270. **Had quite miscarried**: would have been completely lost

271. **upon**: as

272. **advisedly**: knowingly

282-83. **this is like the mending of highways/ In summer**: this is worse than before (theoretically roads should be in good condition in summer weather and the operation of mending them obstructs passage as much as if they were in bad condition).

284. **cuckolds**: betrayed husbands

285. **amazed**: dumfounded

   *Bass.* Portia, forgive me this enforced wrong,
And in the hearing of these many friends
I swear to thee, even by thine own fair eyes,
Wherein I see myself—                    260
   *Por.*              Mark you but that?
In both my eyes he doubly sees himself;
In each eye one. Swear by your double self,
And there's an oath of credit.
   *Bass.*            Nay, but hear me.       265
Pardon this fault, and by my soul I swear
I never more will break an oath with thee.
   *Ant.* I once did lend my body for his wealth,
Which, but for him that had your husband's ring,
Had quite miscarried. I dare be bound again,       270
My soul upon the forfeit, that your lord
Will never more break faith advisedly.
   *Por.* Then you shall be his surety. Give him this,
And bid him keep it better than the other.
   *Ant.* Here, Lord Bassanio. Swear to keep this ring.       275
   *Bass.* By heaven, it is the same I gave the doctor!
   *Por.* I had it of him. Pardon me, Bassanio;
For, by this ring, the doctor lay with me.
   *Ner.* And pardon me, my gentle Gratiano;
For that same scrubbed boy, the doctor's clerk,       280
In lieu of this, last night did lie with me.
   *Gra.* Why, this is like the mending of highways
In summer, where the ways are fair enough.
What, are we cuckolds ere we have deserved it?
   *Por.* Speak not so grossly. You are all amazed.       285
Here is a letter, read it at your leisure;
It comes from Padua from Bellario.
There you shall find that Portia was the doctor,

308. **road:** anchorage

315. **manna:** the food dropped from Heaven to the Israelites, Exodus 16:14-36.

320. **charge us there upon inter'gatories:** compel our answers to your questions (as though under oath in court).

Nerissa there her clerk. Lorenzo here
Shall witness I set forth as soon as you,                   290
And even but now returned. I have not yet
Entered my house. Antonio, you are welcome,
And I have better news in store for you
Than you expect. Unseal this letter soon.
There you shall find three of your argosies              295
Are richly come to harbor suddenly.
You shall not know by what strange accident
I chanced on this letter.
    *Ant.*        I am dumb.
    *Bass.* Were you the doctor, and I knew you not?      300
    *Gra.* Were you the clerk that is to make me cuckold?
    *Ner.* Ay, but the clerk that never means to do it,
Unless he live until he be a man.
    *Bass.* Sweet Doctor, you shall be my bedfellow.
When I am absent, then lie with my wife.                 305
    *Ant.* Sweet lady, you have given me life and living;
For here I read for certain that my ships
Are safely come to road.
    *Por.*         How now, Lorenzo?
My clerk hath some good comforts too for you.          310
    *Ner.* Ay, and I'll give them him without a fee.
There do I give to you and Jessica,
From the rich Jew, a special deed of gift,
After his death, of all he dies possessed of.
    *Lor.* Fair ladies, you drop manna in the way          315
Of starved people.
    *Por.*      It is almost morning,
And yet I am sure you are not satisfied
Of these events at full. Let us go in,
And charge us there upon inter'gatories,                 320
And we will answer all things faithfully.

**329. So sore: so sorely, intensely**

*Gra.* Let it be so. The first inter'gatory
That my Nerissa shall be sworn on is,
Whether till the next night she had rather stay,
Or go to bed now, being two hours to day.          325
But were the day come, I should wish it dark
Till I were couching with the doctor's clerk.
Well, while I live I'll fear no other thing
So sore as keeping safe Nerissa's ring.

                                        *Exeunt.*

# KEY TO

## *Famous Lines and Phrases*

In sooth, I know not why I am so sad.  [*Antonio*—I. i. 1]

I hold the world but as the world . . .
A stage, where every man must play a part,
And mine a sad one.  [*Antonio*—I. i. 80-82]

Let me play the fool  [*Gratiano*—I. i. 83]

"I am Sir Oracle,
And when I ope my lips, let no dog bark!"
[*Gratiano*—I. i. 97-98]

Gratiano speaks an infinite deal of nothing  [*Bassanio*—I. i. 118]

By my troth, Nerissa, my little body is aweary of this great
world.  [*Portia*—I. ii. 1-2]

It is a good divine that follows his own instructions.
[*Portia*—I. ii. 13-14]

God made him, and therefore let him pass for a man.
[*Portia*—I. ii. 52-53]

The devil can cite Scripture for his purpose.  [*Antonio*—I. iii. 98]

It is a wise father that knows his own child.
[*Launcelot*—II. ii. 70-71]

Truth will come to light . . . in the end truth will out.
[*Launcelot*—II. ii. 72-74]

But love is blind, and lovers cannot see
The pretty follies that themselves commit.  [*Jessica*—II. vi. 37-38]

# Key to Famous Lines and Phrases

All that glisters is not gold  [Scroll–II. vii. 66]

Now what news on the Rialto?  [Solanio–III. i. 1]

Hath not a Jew eyes?  [Shylock–III. i. 52 ff]

Tell me, where is fancy bred  [Song–III. ii. 65]

Yes, truly; for look you, the sins of the father are to be laid
upon the children.  [Launcelot–III. v. 1-2]

I am a tainted wether of the flock,
Meetest for death.  [Antonio–IV. i. 117-118]

I never knew so young a body with so old a head.
[Letter–IV. i. 165-166]

The quality of mercy is not strained . . .  [Portia–IV. i. 189]

The moon shines bright. In such a night as this
[Lorenzo–V. i. 1]

How sweet the moonlight sleeps upon this bank!
[Lorenzo–V. i. 62]

I am never merry when I hear sweet music.  [Jessica–V. i. 77]

The man that hath no music in himself . . .
Is fit for treasons, stratagems, and spoils  [Lorenzo–V. i. 91-93]

How far that little candle throws his beams!
So shines a good deed in a naughty world.  [Portia–V. i. 98-99]

. . . the moon sleeps with Endymion,
And would not be awaked.  [Portia–V. i. 117-118]